HENDRIX

TARA LEE
DL GALLIE

Edited by **Lisa Edwards, More Than Words Proofreading**

Proofread by **Karen Hrdlicka, Barren Acres Editing**

Cover Designed by **Tara Lee**

Interior formatting by **DL Gallie**

TRIGGER WARNING

This book mentions a sexual assault and there is a scene dealing with the aftermath of an assault, not sexual. These scenes are not graphic but they do allude to what did occur.
If these scenarios are triggering, we suggest proceeding with caution.

The Lords rule supreme. They're cruel, reckless, and crave the power their status brings.
Their world is corrupt—filled with lies and secrets.
They rule Crestwood Prep like their fathers before them, but nothing lasts forever.
Secrets are about to spill free, lies uncovered.
The Lords aren't as invincible as they once thought.
Let The Games Begin.

This is our school, our kingdom.

My brothers and I rule; we are The Lords.

Secrets run riot through the halls, and I thought I was immune.

And I was, until her—Quinn Ellis.

A positive test changed everything, but I manned up and stood by her side, even when I didn't have to.

Little did either of us know, we were in for another surprise.

Nothing is as it seems, and when all is revealed, our lives will change forever.

QUINN

"FUCK ME HARDER," I demand as I look over my shoulder at Hendrix. His fingers are digging into my hips tightly, no doubt leaving bruises … again. His cock slams in and out of me, getting deeper with each thrust. His head is thrown back, and he gives himself over to the pleasure. He hits that magical spot with each forward movement of his hips. No one fucks like Hendrix Vanderbelt, and I'm a whore for his cock.

"You want it harder, baby?" he asks, his voice deep and gravelly.

"Yes," I mewl, "fuck me harder, Hendrix."

"Yes, ma'am," he responds, and his thrusts become deeper, faster, and harder.

His cock hits deep inside me, no doubt bruising my cervix and marking me as his. My vision begins to dot as the pleasure builds within. He slides a finger into my ass, and that's the detonation I need. I scream his name out at the top of my lungs as my orgasm explodes. My body tingles from head to toe, and the most intense release of my life envelops me. He pulls out and sprays his release all over my ass.

"Fuck, that was close," he pants after he finishes.

"Shit, did you not wrap it?" I ask as I roll onto my back and stare up at him.

"Sorry, got caught up in the moment."

"It's fine, it takes two to tango."

"And we tango the best tango there is," he cockily says, winking at me.

"That we do, Hendrix, that we do."

And like every time we hook up, he pulls his clothes back on, kisses me on the lips, and leaves.

This works for us, and I'm okay with it. We'd fucking kill one another if we dated and I can't go to prison. Yes, I rock orange but those jumpsuits will do nothing for my figure and I'm all about the D. I've only eaten lady taco once but that was enough for me to know, I'm all for the D.

Especially Hendrix's.

As far as penises, peni, what's the plural for penis? Grammar aside, Hendrix's penis is a masterpiece and right now, that's all I need. I don't need a relationship and feelings, therefore, this thing we have going on is perfect. He scratches my itch, I scratch his and then we can go on our merry little way.

My arrangement with Hendrix is one of the reasons I

didn't go to school in Paris. I was accepted earlier this year to a prestigious art school, but when push came to shove, I couldn't leave. If I'm honest, a part of me not going was due to Hendrix, not that I'd ever admit it out loud. His ego is big enough as it is, he is one of the reigning Lords at Crestwood. I don't buy into that pompous bullshit he and his brothers pull, but to get freaky between the sheets with him, I put up with his shit.

Climbing off my bed, I wrap a fluffy orange towel around me—and rock it—then grab my robe and my shower things. Slipping my feet into my slippers, I make my way to the girls' bathroom.

Stepping into the shower stall that's unofficially become mine, I turn on the faucets and wait for the water to heat. Once it's hot, I step under the spray and moan. The hot water feels amazing on my muscles, especially after a vigorous fucking with Hendrix. My whole body begins to tingle as I think back on what went down just before. How I can be randy and ready to go again is beyond me because the things that man can do between the sheets should be illegal.

Glancing down, I see the tattoo on my left hip and, like always, it gives me strength. It's of Medusa. I got the tattoo a few weeks ago to symbolize my strength and survival after my assault earlier this year.

No one here knows what happened, well, my therapist does, but it's my secret to hold on to. I don't want people's pity or sympathy. I want people to see me as the strong woman I am. If I can overcome that on my own, I know I can overcome anything thrown my way because I'm Quinn-fucking-Ellis.

It's funny, being with Hendrix has helped me too.

The first time we had sex after the assault, I locked

myself in the bathrooms after he left and cried until I had no more tears left, but each time after that, it became easier and easier. It was almost like he knew what I needed and helped heal me from the inside out. Then one day, I enjoyed sex again. My therapist still thinks having sex again so soon will be detrimental to my recovery, but she's wrong. I'm stronger because of it.

Finishing up my shower, I get changed and decide to grab a late dinner from the cafeteria, but when I walk downstairs, I see Hudson with a girl in his arms. My eyes rake over the girl, and I immediately know something bad has happened and I'm thrust back to that night. "What the fuck?" I mumble to myself, and my voice garners his attention. He's distraught, and I can tell he's unsure what to do so I immediately jump into action. "What can I do to help?" I ask.

"Can you help me get my sister cleaned up?"

Nodding, I step closer and hold back the gasp wanting to slip out. She looks so broken, and I'm once again assaulted with memories of when I was like her. Realizing we're gaining spectators, I whisper, "Follow me."

He nods and follows me upstairs to the girls' floor. I head straight for the bathrooms. Opening the door, I see two juniors at the mirror. "Out," I growl at the girls at the sink. One of them opens her mouth to protest, but when they see Hudson and the girl, their eyes widen and they quickly scamper away, leaving us alone.

The door clicks closed, and Hudson places the girl down on the ottoman in the middle of the room. Her eyes widen and dart around as she takes everything in. "Hey," he offers, dropping down next to her. "You're safe here, Lauren. Quinn here is going to help me get you cleaned up."

She nods and Hudson steps back, allowing me to take over. He leans against the vanity and watches.

"Hey, Lauren," I whisper. "I'm Quinn. How about we get you into the shower and freshen up?"

She nods and I help her up and into the shower stall. Reaching in, I turn the faucet on and help her undress. She stares into space but winces when I lift her shirt over her head. "Were you …?" I don't finish that sentence, but she shakes her head without having to voice it. *Thank fuck for that*, she wasn't raped, but from the state of her body, she *was* viciously attacked.

She steps under the water, and I step out, giving her some privacy. Walking over to Hudson, the sound of her sobs echo through the room.

"How is she?" Hudson asks, but how do I answer that? So, I just shrug and I see the question in his eyes.

Quickly I shake my head. "She wasn't raped if that's what you're asking." Relief washes over him. "She's shaken up, but she'll be fine, trust me, I know." My eyes widen at that slipped revelation, as do his. "Forget you heard that," I quickly say, and he nods. I don't know Hudson all that well, but from what I do know, I'm positive he'll keep my secret.

Taking the focus off me, I turn it back to Lauren. "Do you have any clothes your sister can wear?"

"Yeah, I'll go grab some things for her." Looking at the shower, he sadly stares at the door and then leaves.

"Lauren, you okay?" I ask a few moments after Hudson leaves.

"I don't know."

"I know the feeling, but I can tell you, it does get easier."

"You were attacked?" she asks.

"A few months back." I pause and take a deep breath. "I ... I was raped," I tell her. This is the first time I have spoken to anyone who wasn't my therapist or a police officer, and it feels good to be able to voice it without breaking down, even if I did tell her through a closed shower door.

The door opens and Lauren stands there, wrapped in my towel. She steps to me and hugs me. "I'm so sorry."

"Don't be, you didn't rape me."

"But—"

"But nothing," I forcefully state. "Whoever raped me is the one who needs to apologize. Not you."

"How are you so strong?"

"Therapy," I tell her, but to be honest, I don't know where my strength comes from. I think to an extent Hendrix is my light. He wants me for me, there's no bullshit. I love that he treats me with respect while at the same time, blowing my mind in every way possible. He erased *his* memory from my body and replaced it with insurmountable pleasure. I own my body. I own my vagina, and no man will ever take that from me again.

Sitting back on the ottoman, silence envelops us, but it doesn't last long because Hudson returns with her things. He smiles brightly at his sister, and she stares blankly at him. "You look good in orange," he tells her, "but let's stick to towels and not prison jumpsuits." Lauren smiles at his joke, but it doesn't reach her eyes.

"I think she'd rock one," I say, trying to lighten the moment. "You, on the other hand, Hudson, could not rock the orange. Plus, you're too pretty for jail. You'd become someone's bitch for sure."

Then I lift up the brush and she nods. Stepping behind her, I begin to brush Lauren's hair. "More like he'd make someone HIS bitch," Lauren adds.

"Seems you and I have different opinions when it comes to your brother. I see him more as a lover than a fighter," I tell them.

"When it comes to those he loves, he's a fighter all the way. He—" But the conversation is halted when the door flies open. It slams into the wall with a bang, shaking and rattling, and I'm surprised it doesn't fall off its hinges. Lauren flinches and leans back into me, cowering in fear. We all turn our heads and see Reign standing in the doorway.

"Out," I growl at him, but the dickhead just stands there, his gaze flickering between the three of us. His fists are clenched and he's angry, what the fuck for I have no clue. "Get out, Vanderbelt," I sneer at him again.

"What's going on?" Alani says as she appears behind Reign. Her sudden appearance confuses me, I thought she was with Hudson, but she's here with Reign? This is all *Days of Our Livesesque.*

"Nothing," the three of us all state at once.

"Right, nothing," Reign spits. His face is red with anger and his jaw is clenched, like his fists. His gaze keeps flicking from Hudson to Lauren to me. He's about to say something else when Alani tugs his arm. "Come with me," she says, but he just stands there. His eyes are locked on Lauren. "Now, Vanderbelt," Alani growls, and I find myself smiling at my friend. For a wee little thing, Alani Thomas is a spitfire, a redheaded spitfire. She pulls again on Reign's arm and this time, he follows her.

A few seconds later, she darts back and gives Hudson a look that confuses me even more.

"She likes you," Lauren says, bumping her brother's shoulder, and then under her breath adds, "he does too."

"Me too," Hudson mutters in reply. Lauren's and my

eyes widen as it sinks in, he's referring to them both. Oh. My. Fucking. God, the three of them are getting it on together.

How does no one know this?

This is the best gossip of the year, even better than Arlen returning from the dead.

Hudson and Lauren chat about where she's going to stay tonight and they settle on his room. We pack up and as we walk toward the exit, Lauren mumbles, "Can't believe I'm saying this, but I can't wait to go back to New York. I fucking hate this town."

To an extent, I agree with her. Crestwood sucks but it's my home. I grew up here, and some of my favorite memories are from living here. I hope one day, Lauren will realize one event does not dictate your future.

HENDRIX

QUINN LEFT yesterday for New York, and I'll never admit this out loud, but I fucking miss her. Okay, I mostly miss her pussy and what it does to me, but there's also a small part of me that misses Quinn, the person. She is unlike anyone I've ever met before. Yes, she comes across as bitchy at times. What chick doesn't? But once you get to know her, really get to know her, she's an amazing person.

"Are you still moping?" Saint asks, sinking into the chair beside me and kicking me with his foot. I growl, giving him a sideways glare. "Geez, Quinn's got you growly." He laughs.

"Who's growly?" Thatcher asks as he walks into the room.

Saint hitches his thumb toward me.

"When isn't Hendrix in a mood?" Reign states, coming in behind Thatch.

"Enough," I snap, "fuck."

"Oookay, someone needs to get laid," Reign jokes.

"Says the man getting in on tap from two people," Saint reminds us.

A few days ago, our brother confessed his deepest darkest secret. He's bi and in a throuple relationship with Alani Thomas and Hudson Finley. We couldn't be happier for him. For a long time there he was lost, and it was because he was hiding who he really is, but now it's all out in the open he's so much happier and we finally have our brother back.

"I don't know why I put up with you fuckers," I mutter under my breath, but of course, my brothers hear me.

"Triplets," both Saint and Thatcher say out loud together, causing them to laugh.

Reign shakes his head tapping my arm. "Come on, you know we're just busting your balls, 'cause, well, you never mope. It's fucking weird to see you moping," he says, gaining Thatcher's and Saint's attention.

"Yeah, bro, I mean, you and Quinn aren't even official," Saint says. "What gives?"

I want to be, I almost say out loud but keep it to myself because I keep fucking up where Quinn is concerned. *Fuck,* why is this so hard? I like her. She likes me. And the sex, holy fucking porno man. She and her pussy can bring me to my knees.

Shaking off my mopey mood, the four of us shoot the

shit for a while and when the conversation lulls, I return to sulking over Quinn.

Saint slaps my leg, pushes himself up, and looks at my brothers. "Come on, let's leave him be before he goes all Hulk on us."

They both nod, and then Saint ushers Thatcher and Reign out, leaving me alone with my thoughts of Quinn and what I want for us.

I've tried calling Quinn multiple times today with no success. I'm frustrated as all hell and acting like Thatcher, being all growly and moody. The need to hear her voice is strong, and it's confusing because what we have isn't a relationship. We fuck and move on, but lately, I find myself wanting more with her … and I get the feeling she wants more too but, like me, she's scared to voice it aloud so we dance around it. Maybe when she gets back from the Big Apple, I need to take her out on a date. A proper date with flowers and a restaurant.

Not coming up with any specific ideas, I decide to call it a night. Popping my phone on the bedside table, I climb under the covers and promptly drift off to sleep.

A loud ringing disturbs my sleep, and I groan in frustration, I was having the best dream. Quinn was on her knees … ohh, right, my phone. Rolling over, I grab my phone from my side table and smile when I see Quinn's name and picture, lighting up the screen.

"Quinn?" I answer, sitting myself up.

"Hendrix," her voice comes out muffled and then she's silent.

"Quinn," I repeat. Fear begins to build, and that intensifies when she makes a strange noise in the back of her throat. There's that same muffled sound from before and then I hear it, she's crying. *Fuck.* "Quinn," I murmur, "what's wrong?"

"I'm sorry," she whispers, her voice so quiet I almost miss it.

"Sorry?" I repeat, *what's she talking about?* "For what, baby?"

"I'm sorry, I … I have to go," she mutters, and before I can ask her what the fuck is going on, the line goes dead.

"Fuck," I hiss into the empty room.

Stabbing at her name again, my call goes unanswered. As do the fifty million other ones as I try Quinn again and again and again.

"What the fuck have you got yourself into, Quinn?" I mumble when I once again get her voicemail.

Eventually, I fall asleep, but for the rest of the weekend I'm unable to focus, and as Rian reminds me, "I'm acting like Thatcher before Remy arrived."

The thought that something terrible has happened to Quinn plays on repeat. I can't concentrate so I hit her name again and wait as it rings.

"Hendrix," her soft voice murmurs through the line.

She sounds broken, but I'm so relieved to hear her voice. "Quinn, baby, are you okay?" I grimace when I realize the word 'baby' slipped out before I could stop it.

A soft gasp breaks free, and the last thing I hear before the line goes dead is a broken sob.

Fuck.

After that, Quinn sends all my calls to voicemail and

I'm on the edge, waiting for her to come home because whatever happened in New York is something we need to talk about.

The need to demand she tell me what the fuck is going on is so damn strong, but I know I need to keep my cool, I can't push her. We're not a couple, we've never been one. We're just, I guess the best word to describe us is fuck buddies, but I want to change that. Maybe this is my chance to show her I'm more than just a good-looking guy with a dick who can bring her unsurmountable pleasure. Maybe I can show her I'm a man you bring home to your parents. A man who will love you unconditionally. I know I sound like a pussy, or Thatcher with Remy, but Quinn is worth it. She's fucking worth it.

The moment she steps into the cafeteria, I look up, and as soon as my eyes land on her, I can feel the change in her and our, whatever the fuck we have going on. Our eyes lock and before I can take a step toward her, she turns away, fleeing from the cafeteria.

"What the fuck?" I growl, and without thinking I take off after her.

I'm not done.

No, we're not done. Not yet … I hope.

QUINN

WHEN I WALK into the cafeteria for dinner and see Hendrix, the urge to flee slammed into me light a freight train. I'd managed to avoid him all day and I was hoping he would have had a late dinner tonight but no, he's here but I can't be here when he is. So, like the coward I am, I turn on my heel and run. But I should have known better. The way he blew my phone up this weekend should have alluded to the fact that as soon as I got back, we'd be having words, but I can't do it. I feel so guilty. I never should have gone to New York. Sure, I got to catch up with Lauren and see firsthand that she's doing well after her attack, but I should have never gone to that club on Saturday night with her and Risa. If I had just stayed at the hotel, I wouldn't have made the biggest mistake of my life …

… *Lauren, Risa, and I have just stepped into Belissimo, a new trendy club that has opened up around the corner from where Risa lives. Lauren and I stopped in to visit her after we had lunch at Tavern on the Green. I always visit there when I'm in New York, it's my favorite restaurant in the city. I fell in love with it when I was twelve, and my grandma and grandpa took me there for dinner before we went to a show on Broadway. After that first visit, I was in love. All the fairy lights reminded me of a secret fairy garden. Combine that with the dress my grandparents bought me that day, and I felt like a princess and that feeling hits every time I visit. In the waaaay distant future, my daughter and I will get all dressed up and I will take her there too and, hopefully, she will fall in love with the place like I did.*

As soon as we walk into Belissimo, my body starts to sway to the beat of the music. My body doesn't bend and move like Ri's and Lauren's do, you can tell the two of them are dancers. It's mesmerizing watching them. I made a promise to Lauren to come back and see their show in a few months' time because they are both very talented dancers. I can see why they attend Stepz.

The three of us dance and dance and dance but unlike the professionals, after four songs, I'm exhausted and need a drink, so I make my way to the bar.

Yes, I'm only eighteen, but I look much older, and the barman doesn't even bat an eyelid 'cause his eyes are locked on my tits. Typical male. I order myself a cosmo, I am in New York after all, and when it's placed in front of me, I take that first sip and moan. This is one hell of a cocktail.

Ri and Lauren join me, and after a few cocktails, Lauren decides shots are in order. She orders a round of tequila shots and three shots later, I'm past tipsy, but I'm not drunk-drunk, yet.

Needing to use the ladies', I excuse myself and make my way to the restrooms. After peeing, I wash my hands and when I step out into the corridor, I bump into a hard body. When I look up, I smile. "Hendrix," I slur.

"You can call me whatever you want, baby," he says, sliding his hand around my waist. His voice is squeakier than I remember, but when he squeezes my ass, all thoughts of his voice evaporate. "Wanna get out of here, baby?"

"I'm with Lauren and Ri."

"So, say goodbye and then let's go."

Nodding, I take his hand and make my way over to the girls. "Look who I found," I singsong when I reach them. Lauren looks confused, but Ri smiles at Hendrix behind me. "I'm going to head out with him." I flick my thumb behind me. "Don't wait up." I wink at them, but before I pull away, Lauren grabs my wrist.

"Are you sure?"

Nodding, I smile at her. "I'm sure. I'm going to get laid and then I'll bring breakfast with me tomorrow."

"As long as you're sure."

"I'll be fine," I tell her. "Nothing to worry about."

Yeah, nothing to worry about. Famous last words. You see, in my inebriated state, I thought the guy I took home was Hendrix, but it wasn't. In my drunken fog, I mistook Jim for my man Hendrix, and that night, I made the biggest mistake of my life. I cheated on Hendrix with a guy who in the sober light of day looks nothing like Hendrix. He's just a guy named Jim. I cheated with a guy named Jim. At least he could have had a cool name like Jameson, but no, I slept with a Jim. He let me have my mini freak-out and got me a coffee when he asked what I needed. In my freaked-out state, I decided caffeine was what I needed while freaking out I slept with a Hendrix look-alike named Jim and not the real Hendrix 'cause the real Hendrix is back in Crestwood.

I know Hendrix and I aren't official or anything and we're just fucking, but since he and I have been fooling around, I have only slept with him and in one night, I ruined what Hendrix and I had been building because we have been building something. It isn't just sex for us anymore, it's a relationship, just without the label. I mean, when you are just fooling around with someone, you don't know they love their mom unconditionally. Or they eat their sides before their main meal. Or how he doesn't like peanuts but he loves super crunchy peanut butter. Or he would love to be a deep sea diver, but he's petrified of running out of air while underwater. You don't know those things about a random hookup, you know those things about someone you are dating and, now, I can never sleep with him again because I'm a whore.

"Quinn, wait up," he shouts after me, but I can't look at him. I quicken my pace, but his strides are much bigger than mine, and he reaches me before I can slink away into the night.

He grips my wrist and spins me to face him, and when I look up into his hazel eyes, I feel like I want to be sick. Pulling away from him, I turn to the side and throw up into the flower bed beside us. Everything in my stomach comes up and when there's nothing left, I just make gagging sounds. I wish I could vomit away the guilt, but I can't. And that guilt builds further when Hendrix holds my dark locks back and rubs my back in circles in that soothing kind of way.

In that boyfriend kind of way.

Him being so nice causes me to break down. Falling to my knees, I cover my face and sob into my hands.

"Quinn, babe, what's wrong?"

"I ... I ..." But I can't form words. Sobs wrack my body. Breathing becomes difficult. My vision begins to dot.

I need to get away from him.

I need to get out of here.

Pulling myself away from him, I stand up and take two steps, but from vomiting, sobbing, and not breathing properly, I don't get very far. Everything turns black, my body goes lax, and I begin to fall.

HENDRIX

ONE MINUTE I'm rubbing circles on Quinn's back, and the next, she's pulling away and falling. Reaching out, I catch her before she hits the ground. Scooping her into my arms, I make my way to the dormitory wing and up to her room. Along the way, I bump into Remy. "What happened?"

"I don't know. She ran away from me, started vomiting, and then she fainted."

"Is she okay?"

"I don't know. Can you help me get her into bed?"

Remy nods and walks ahead of me. "Keys?" she demands when we reach Quinn's room.

"Pocket? Maybe," I answer.

Remy digs into Quinn's pocket and pulls out her phone. Then she digs in the other one when I shuffle her in my arms, and she finds her keys. Unlocking the door, she opens it, flicks on the light, and steps aside for me to enter.

Walking in, I gently place Quinn on top of her hideous orange duvet. Orange has to be the ugliest color there is, but Quinn Ellis is obsessed with the color … and some-how, she rocks it and makes it less hideous. She is seri-ously the only person I know who could rock an orange prison jumpsuit.

Remy stands above us as I brush a tendril of hair off her face. "Can you get some water for when she wakes up?"

Rem nods and races out, leaving me alone with Quinn. She's pale, very pale, and I'm extremely worried about her. The room is really bright with the overhead light on, so I switch on the bedside lamp and turn off the main one.

Sitting back on the edge of the bed, I take her hand in mine. Bringing it to my lips, I kiss her knuckles. "What's going on with you?" I whisper, continuing to stare down at a still-unconscious Quinn.

Remy returns with some water and a wet washcloth. Taking it from her, I pat it over Quinn's face before wiping at her mouth, removing some dried vomit. She begins to stir, and when I see her eyelids flutter, relief fills my body. "Quinn, baby, open your eyes for me."

At the sound of my voice, her eyes fly open. She stares up at me, her eyes wide and full of confusion. Her mouth opens and closes, but nothing comes out and then her eyes well with tears. She lets out a guttural sob and rolls to her side, facing away from me and curling into a ball.

"Please, Quinn," I beg, "tell me what's wrong."

"I want to be alone," she blubbers.

"Well, too fucking bad, I'm not leaving you alone like this. You collapsed just now and I'm worried about you."

"Just go, I'm fine."

"Quinn—" I try again, but Remy places her hand on my shoulder and squeezes tightly. Lifting my gaze to hers, I see a 'shut the fuck up' look on her face.

"Quinn," she softly says her name. "It's Remy, what can I do?"

"Make him go … please."

"I'm …" I don't finish what I was going to say when I see the intense look on Rem's face. She nods toward the door and raises her eyebrows at me, seems she's adopted Thatcher's 'do as you're told' look. I don't want to leave Quinn like this, but I also know she doesn't want me here and I don't want to upset her any more than she already is. "Fine," I relent, my tone harsh but I don't give a rat's ass. "I'm going, but Remy has to stay."

"Fine," Quinn agrees but still refuses to look at me.

Leaning down, I press my lips to her head. She gasps at the contact but still doesn't turn toward me. "We'll talk tomorrow," I tell her, and when I stand up and walk out of her room, Remy follows me.

"You'll stay with her?" I ask when we step out into the corridor.

She nods. "I will."

"And you'll tell me what you find out?"

"I will, BUT if she tells me not to tell you, then girl code dictates that I don't."

"Fuck girl code," I growl. "I need to know she's okay."

"She will be, she's Quinn-fucking-Ellis." I smile at that because she's right. Quinn is the strongest person I know. She's feisty and strong, but at the same time, she's soft and caring. In other words, she's perfect.

"You're right, but— "

"She will tell you whatever is going on when she's ready. Don't push her or me. Now, go do whatever it is you do on a Sunday night."

"I'd normally be doing Quinn, but that's clearly not gonna happen tonight."

Remy shakes her head. "Just go." She turns her back to me and slips back into Quinn's room, closing the door behind her.

Not wanting to leave them alone, I cross the hall and slide down the wall across from her room. Stretching my legs out, I cross my arms and stare intently at the door. I can hear soft murmurs coming from the other side and wish I could hear what they're saying, but hearing them nattering eases my worry slightly because it means Quinn is opening up to Remy.

I just wish she'd talk to me.

QUINN

"YOU OKAY?" Remy asks as she reenters my room alone. That shocks me 'cause Hendrix is OTT alpha and I was sure he was going to swing his dick around and demand to be here.

Shrugging at her, I try my best to stop my bottom lip from trembling, but the moment is short-lived, and it begins to shake uncontrollably as tears cascade down my face.

"Quinn?" Remy says my name like a question before she places her hand on my shoulder and squeezes, reassuring me that she's here for me. If I'm honest, I wish it was Rowan here but she's got shit of her own going on right now that she being tight-lipped about, so I guess Remy will do.

"I-I screwed up." Wiping the tears from my cheeks and eyes, I watch as Remy waits for me to continue, but if I say it out loud it will reiterate the truth, and I fucking hate what happened.

I

Fucking

Hate

It

"Look, Quinn, I know we're not that close, but if there's anything you want to talk about, I'm here."

"I cheated on Hendrix," I blurt out before another round of sobs wracks through my body.

"Oh, Quinn," she murmurs softly. She sits on the bed next to me and places her hand on my knee, squeezing in that reassuring kind of way, but it does little to reassure me. When Hendrix finds out, he'll walk away from me forever, and the thought of that guts me.

"How? What happened?" she asks.

Sitting up, I cross my legs, crisscross applesauce style. Taking a deep breath, I begin, "I was drunk, and I know that's not an excuse, but I thought it was him. I … I don't know why. I mean, he was here in Crestwood, and I was in New York, but I thought he came there for me, and in my drunkenness, I went home with him," I air quote him, "and then in the light of the day, I realized my mistake." Lowering my head, I shake it at myself and my stupidity. Lifting it up, I look over at Remy and I don't see anger, I see hurt. For me. She's hurting for me.

"Quinn," she says softly, squeezing my knee again, "it was a mistake. We all make mistakes and Hendrix will understand. I'm sure he will, and if he's like Thatch, he will have made mistakes too."

"Don't be nice to me," I snap, looking away. I can't handle Remington being nice to me right now. "He's going to hate me when he finds out. He'll probably never talk to me again."

"You don't know that," Remy says. Reaching out, she tucks a tendril of hair that's fallen down behind my ear.

"Don't be stupid, Remington," I groan out loud, jumping to my feet and twisting my sleeves down my hands as I begin pacing my room. "Hendrix is a Lord. He's never made it official with me, but it's always been an unspoken thing between us. I'm his, and he's mine. Once he finds out I slept with someone who isn't him he's going to ruin me," I rush out in one breath, panting the moment I finish.

Cupping my hand in hers, Remy pulls me back to sit on my bed. "I think you need to talk to him, Quinn. Maybe if you explain the situation he might …" I scoff, causing her to look at me with a raised eyebrow.

"Come on," I sneer. "Do you really think Thatcher would understand if it was you?" I snap at her in a bitchy tone. I know she's trying but come on, I fucked another guy. There's no fucking way he'll be like, 'It's all good, babe.'

Her eyes go wide, causing me to laugh a little. "Exactly," I murmur. "I'm fucked and not in a good way."

"Okay, so maybe that was not the best idea I've ever had. What about you seduce him first?" she offers, her mouth turning up on one side. "If you're fucking him, he won't focus on the fact you fucked someone else and all will be okay."

If only it was that simple.

"I ..."

"You have to tell him, Quinn. Ease your mind, and you never know ..."

I know she's right. I have to confess what I did and be prepared for Hendrix to lose his shit. His temper is short on a normal day, but knowing I have to reveal what I did; Hendrix may just go nuclear and even the best blow job in the world couldn't fix this.

Shit, I'm totally screwed.

Remy and I chat for a while longer, and I realize she's a pretty cool chick and I can see why Thatcher fell for her. She's really likable, and I can see us becoming friends, and with that, I have to confess, I could really do with one.

Opening my door, Remy smiles at me before she makes her way toward the boys' dorms and, my guess, to Thatcher's bed. I'm just about to close my door when my eyes widen. My gaze lands on Hendrix sitting across the hall. He's stretched out looking hotter than hot, his eyes burning through me. He gives me one of his famous cocky grins and my stomach turns to knots when I realize that may be the last one I ever get.

"Hey," I murmur softly.

"Hey," he repeats, pushing himself up to his feet. He walks over to me and takes one of my hands in his before he pulls me into him, my chest crashing into his. Wrapping my arms around his waist, I hold on tight.

Pulling back, I stare up at him. He reaches out and grips my face between his palms, and before I can get a word out, his lips crash to mine. His tongue pushes into my mouth and mine slides into his.

Closing my eyes, I savor this kiss before softly murmuring his name, "Hendrix."

"I just want to get lost in you, Quinn. Let me get lost in you, baby."

A sob rips through me at his sweetness. Everything I did crashes into me but knowing soon enough Hendrix will turn away from me, I grip his jaw and take his lips once more.

Once more and then I can confess.

Tugging on his hand, we move into my room. Hendrix kicks the door closed and lifts me, throwing me onto my bed before ripping my clothes off in double time, not giving me a chance to protest, not that I would.

"I fucking need you, Quinn," he growls.

"I need you too," I reply.

Lifting to my elbows, he leans down, and my lips brush against his while his cock presses into me.

Deciding to keep my secret for one more night, I let Hendrix have me one last time because come tomorrow, I'll lose the one person I've always needed. The one person I've been too scared to admit my feelings for out loud.

Why did I go to New York?

Like usual with us, we fuck and then when I'm passed out, he slinks out of my room like a thief in the night. I don't know if I'm relieved or pissed when I wake up alone, but I do know the next time I see him, I need to come clean, but of course, like the chickenshit I am, I do everything I can to avoid him.

HENDRIX

QUINN IS AVOIDING me and it's really starting to piss me off.

It's been a few weeks since I found her and left her with Remy. Meaning it's been a few weeks since I was inside her and I'm ready to bust a nut because Quinn's pussy is the only pussy I need or want.

If she sees me in the corridor or cafeteria, she takes off like Speedy-freaking-Gonzales. And Remy is still tight-lipped and won't tell me what's going on. My mind is running all over the place with different scenarios, and I have no clue if I should be worried or not.

But for now, I have other things to worry about. I thought finding out Reign was bi and is in a throuple relationship with Alani and Hudson was huge news, but finding out that Arlen Hearst killed our dad takes the icing on the cake. I'm not upset Dad is dead, no one is, but it pains me to see my brother hurting over who did kill him because by pure chance, Reign found Arlen with the gun that killed Dad, and now the fucker is in hiding.

"Still no answer?" Saint asks Reign. Alani and Hudson are missing and no one can reach them.

Reign shakes his head and seeing him so distraught hurts. I'd do anything for my brothers and right now, I want to take his pain away, but I can't. And then there's Thatcher, he and his big mouth have fucked things up with Remy so I now have two brothers to worry about. Thankfully, Saint is okay and I fucking hope it stays that way.

"I don't need this right now, Saint," Reign snaps. Seems while I was in my head thinking about all the shit happening, Saint and Reign got into it.

"What do you mean?" Saint asks, playing dumb and infuriating our brother further.

"This … this big brother crap," Reign sneers. "Okay? I don't need you to be a smart-ass. I don't need you to do anything but help me find my boyfriend and girlfriend because I'm telling you, something isn't right. They wouldn't ignore me like this."

Saint realizes he's pushed too far and he knocks Reign's knee. "Hey, it's okay, we'll find them, they have to be somewhere."

He looks to Thatch and me and we nod, reassuring him that we will find them and I really hope I didn't just lie to my brother.

He gets a text, and we all hope it's from one of his partners, but he says it's spam when I ask. I don't believe him, and when his phone lights up again, Thatcher snatches the phone from him.

"Jesus fuck," he snaps, shoving it at me. My eyes widen when I see the screen. He tosses the phone to Saint. "What the fuck, Reign?" Saint growls. "You've been talking to the fucker?"

Another text comes through, and Saint's eyes widen at the screen. He shakes his head before throwing the phone back at Reign, leaving both Thatch and I confused. He shows us the phone and Thatch sees red.

"I need to go to them, I need to …" He goes to get up, but Thatcher stops him.

"Reign, you need to go into this with a level head. Arlen is dangerous."

"Hhhh … he won't hurt me." Even as the words pass through Reign's lips, none of us believe him and I'm positive he doesn't believe his own words.

"Bullshit," Saint barks. "He's a fucking psycho killer and kidnapper. No fucking way are you going alone. No. Fucking. Way."

"I'm going," he growls.

"That's a bad fucking idea," I growl.

"Please, I need to go. Alone, I need to save them. I won't survive if they get hurt because of me."

Seeing my brother fall apart guts me, mind you, if Quinn had been taken, I'd be losing my shit like he is too. Saint and I look to Thatcher, as the oldest he's like our unofficial leader, not that we'd ever admit that out loud. His head is big enough as it is but proving my point, Thatcher speaks and takes charge. "Fine, but before you go, we're going to come up with a plan. I'm not sending you to your fucking death, Reign."

"Fine," he murmurs, shocking me that he's giving in so easily, but then again, he knows Arlen better than all of us. We discuss our options, and when we have our plan, we head off to rescue Alani and Hudson.

QUINN

THIS PLACE IS GETTING MORE and more fucked up by the day. Just when I think it can't get any crazier, it does. After my attack earlier this year, I should have left. I should have gone to that school in Paris like Mom wanted me to, but no, I was fooled by a boy.

A boy who I was falling for.

A boy who puts up with my shit and still wants to be around me.

A boy who has an amazing heart, a beautiful soul, and a tongue that is magical. The things Hendrix Vanderbelt can do with his tongue are everything a girl could ever want, but after I fucked up with a boy who looked like the boy I was falling for, I will never get to feel the pleasure his tongue can bring ever again.

Those memories evaporate when I bump into someone coming out of the elevator. They reach out and grab me, and a feeling of déjà vu washes over me, leaving me rattled. When I look up and see the dark hood covering their face, I'm transported back to that night. "It's ... it's you," I blubber, "you ... you attacked me." Fear courses through me like it did the night I was attacked.

"Like fuck I did," they growl. Their voice sounds different, but maybe I've distorted it in my mind over time. "You don't even fucking know me."

"It was you. I swear it was. You ... you raped me in that house."

He pushes his hood back, and I come face-to-face with Arlen Hearst. "I didn't fucking touch you. It was that fucker, Brennan." My eyes widen when he says that. "I was trapped in the room next door. I heard it all go down."

My eyes well with tears as I remember the feeling of him, well Brennan, rutting into me. The smell of his breath against my cheek. A lump forms in the back of my throat and I race over to the trash can and vomit. I seem to be doing a lot of that lately. The constant memories of that night and the other night cause me to physically be sick. My therapist said with time, it will ease, but if anything, it's getting worse. *I really should have gone to Paris.* I shake my head and wipe my mouth when a noise from inside one of the apartments garners my attention.

"You hear that?" I ask Arlen.

He shakes his head. "Hear what?" Then I hear it again, and this time, Arlen looks panicked. "I'm glad I could clear up the rape thing for you, but I have to run." Before I can say anything, he unlocks the door across from me, and my eyes widen when I see Alani Thomas tied up on the bed. Her face is red from crying, her hair matted. She looks scared.

"What the fuck?" I mumble, but I should have kept quiet because the sound of my voice causes Arlen to spin on his heel. He stares menacingly at me for a few seconds and then marches over to me. He grabs me around the neck and begins to choke me. I love a good choking, in the sexual kind of way, but this is anything but sexual, and I fear for my safety and life. My vision begins to dot as I scratch at his hands, but he's too strong. He drags me toward the fire escape and opens the door. He stares into my eyes, and I see the moment he decides to end my life. With little effort, he pushes me backward, and I begin to tumble down the stairs. My arms flail about as I fly through the air before landing on my back. Hitting the stairs hard and knocking the wind out of me, I slide down them, coming to a stop on the landing below with a thud. Blinking, I stare up at a smirking Arlen, and his face is the last thing I see before darkness envelops me.

"Ouch," I hiss, rubbing the back of my head. Opening my eyes, it's dark and I don't know where I am. Taking a deep breath, my neck and throat hurt as the oxygen filters into my lungs. Pushing myself up into a sitting position, I think my wrist is broken when I put pressure onto it and it hurts like a bitch. "Fuck me," I complain, and then I remember what I saw.

Pulling my phone out of my pocket, I click on *his* name. It rings, and the asshole sends my call to voicemail. Ending the call, I try again. It rings and rings until I get his voicemail again. "Fucking answer, asshole," I hiss as I call again and like the first time, he sends the call to voicemail. I try one more time and this time he picks up.

"I don't have time for your shit, Quinn," he sneers through the line.

"Fuck you, asshole," I snap at him. "Maybe I shouldn't tell you what I know."

"Just tell me and then fuck off, I'm busy."

It hurts the way he's speaking to me right now, but then again, I deserve it. He and I could be something amazing, but one drunken mistake and I've fucked it all up for us.

"Quinn," he growls, "you have three seconds and then I'm hanging up."

"I know where Arlen is."

"So do we," he snaps at me. "He's about to meet with Reign in the cemetery."

"Ahhhh, he's not at the cemetery. He's at the Crestwood Central Apartments on the fifth floor and he has Alani. I saw him after visiting—"

"The fuck you just say?"

"Arlen, he's here at Crestwood Central and he has Alani."

"Is Hudson there too?"

"I didn't see him."

"Fuck," he hisses. "What the fuck are you doing at Crestwood Central Apartments? And how did this happen?"

"I was visiting … it doesn't matter who I was visiting, but I bumped into him in the hallway an—"

"Stay the fuck away from him, he's a fucking psycho."

"I know. He pushed me down a flight of stairs when I saw Alani in his room."

"He hurt you?" The softness in his voice is a complete one-eighty from only seconds ago, reminding me of the soft and loving Hendrix. "Are you okay?"

"I think my wrist is broken and he choked me—"

"Bet you liked that," he teases.

"No, I did not. I only like it when broody assholes choke me while their dick is in my ass."

"Fuck, babe, the visions I have right now."

"Focus, dickhead," I snap at him. "The time for that is over and FYI, it's never happening again, but you need to get here now. I'm going to call the police."

"No," he shouts down the line. "Let us handle it. We need to talk to the fucker before he's taken away."

"Why do I get the feeling there's more to this than just him taking Alani?"

"Because there is." He pauses. "Just for once in your fucking life, Quinn, listen to me."

"Fine," I snap, "but can you at least call me an ambulance?"

"No," he snaps, and I'm ready to give him a piece of my mind when he tacks on, "I'll come get you."

Before I can reply, he hangs up. "Thanks," I mutter to myself, once again wishing I'd gone to Paris.

HENDRIX

HOLY FUCK, life here in Crestwood seems to be getting crazier and crazier these days. Thanks to Quinn, we managed to rescue Hudson and Alani from Arlen's clutches and he is now locked away where he can't hurt anyone else. Now Thatcher, Saint, Remy, Grayson, and I are at the hospital, waiting to hear if Hudson is okay.

Remy is beating herself up that her brother isn't who she thought he was, and no matter how many times we tell her none of us knew, it doesn't sink in.

"Hey, how's Quinn?" Saint asks.

"Fuck," I hiss, "I totally forgot about her. The revelation

Arlen was in love with Dad and that's why he killed him has kinda been at the forefront of my mind." Pushing up from my seat, I walk over to the reception desk. Putting on my most flirtatious smile, I look at the woman behind the desk. "Darlene, such a pretty name," I tell her.

"What do you want?" she says, ignoring my flirting. I try smiling again, and she raises her hand. "Look, kid, I'm old enough to be your grandma, just tell me what you want and if I can do it, I will."

A laugh escapes me. "I fucking wish you were my grandma. You're awesome."

"Tell me something I don't know. Now, what can I do for you, sweet cheeks?"

"There's a girl—"

"It's always a girl," she teases.

"Well, this girl, I care for her very much, and I'd like to see if she's okay."

"Name?"

"Quinn Ellis," I tell her.

She punches a few keys on her keyboard and then lifts her gaze back to me. "Bed seven, I'll buzz you through."

"Thanks, Darl." I blow her a kiss and walk to the door, waiting to be buzzed in.

The door beeps and the locks disengage. Pushing on them, I head in. Walking around, I find room seven easily but stop outside the curtain when I hear someone chatting with Quinn, and when I hear what they say, my eyes widen and my heart stutters in my chest. "… we will schedule you an ultrasound later today and then you can see your baby."

Pushing the curtain back, I step into the room. "You're pregnant?"

Both the doctor and Quinn snap their heads toward

me. Quinn's eyes are wide, and I'm not sure if it's in shock because I'm here, because she's pregnant, or both.

"Is it mine?" I ask.

Her mouth opens and closes but she doesn't utter a word. Then she utters three words that shock the fuck out of me. "I don't know." She drops her gaze to her hands, "I-I, Hendrix…" Quinn stutters, twisting her hands in her lap while the doctor's stare continues to flick between the two of us.

Clenching my hands by my sides, my nails dig into my palms as I try to tame the anger building inside me.

She's fucking pregnant.

And didn't tell me.

I know we aren't anything official, but I really thought she'd tell me something important like this. I knew she was a bitch, but this is low, even for her.

"I'll give you two a moment," the doctor says and he quickly exits, closing the curtain behind him as he high-tails it out of here, leaving us alone.

Silence falls across the room.

Quinn is still staring at her hands, she won't even meet my gaze. I watch her as she swallows, her throat bobbing with the action. Her shoulders lift and fall. *Is she crying?*

"Quinn?" I say, my tone is gentler this time.

Wiping at her face—guess she is crying after all. She lifts her head and the tears continue to fall down her cheeks. Our gazes meet and I see the devastation on her face. Without her saying a word, the look on her face tells me everything I need to know, this baby's not mine.

Ripping the curtain open, I storm out with Quinn screaming my name. I should be relieved the bastard isn't mine, but there's a small part of me that for a brief moment was excited at the prospect of being a dad.

The elevator doors open the moment I push the button, and the second I climb inside I feel her behind me, and it's confirmed when she calls out my name, "Hendrix."

Spinning around, Quinn's face comes into view, and we stare at one another as the doors begin to close. The moment the doors shut I lose it. My fist repeatedly slams into the steel wall of the elevator, and I let out a murderous scream.

Dropping my hand down by my side, blood drips down my knuckles and lands on the linoleum floor below, pooling by my feet.

My phone begins to vibrate in my pocket, but I ignore it. I know I should answer, it could be news about Hudson, but I don't want to speak to anyone right now. My emotions are all over the place, and I'm likely to say something I'll regret—I'm not Thatcher, I'm using my brain and removing myself from the situation so I don't do anything stupid.

Realizing the elevator is not moving, I push the button for the ground floor. Leaning against the wall, I tip my head back and try to calm myself before the doors slide open again. The people standing on the other side sense my turmoil and move out of my way, allowing me to exit.

Storming through the lobby, I race through the parking lot and climb into my car. Resting my forehead on the steering wheel, I scream once again, letting out all my frustrations. Today is fucked. One for the history books but I know one thing, even though this baby isn't mine, I'm going to be there for Quinn.

QUINN

SHIT, shit, fucking, shit.

This is so much worse than him finding out I cheated on him. Well, technically, I didn't cheat because we aren't official, but I slept with someone else. Ergo, I cheated.

Dropping to my knees in the middle of the hospital corridor, I fall apart. Tears streak down my cheeks, and my heart breaks that he left.

I'm all alone.

Pregnant and alone … and currently barefoot as I'm in the hospital. *Can I get anymore cliché?*

A nurse stops beside me and helps me up. "He wasn't

meant to find out like this," I blubber as she escorts me back to my cubicle.

Climbing onto the bed, I lie on my back and stare up at the ceiling, absentmindedly rubbing my stomach as the tears wrack my body. The nurse doesn't utter a word to me as she goes about her business. When I shiver, she silently grabs the blanket and covers my body with the scratchy material. She squeezes my ankle reassuringly and then leaves … just like Hendrix did.

He's gone.

Rolling to my side, I bring my knees up to my chest and hug them as tears continue to fall down my face. The last thing I remember before my eyes grow heavy is Hendrix is gone, and I've lost him forever.

I'm startled awake when a new person is in my room, and there's a machine behind her. "Hi," she says. "I'm assisting Dr. Paige. Let's have a look at your baby."

Nodding, I roll to my back like the technician asks. I lift my gown and she chuckles, "During your first trimester, we do a transvaginal ultrasound."

My eyes widen cause that doesn't sound comfortable, or safe. "I promise it's safe for your baby but it might be a little uncomfortable."

Nodding, I lay back on the bed and follow her instructions for the scan.

My eyes are glued to the screen. Everything looks like a blurry mess to me. She points out my baby and I lift my bandaged—not broken just sprained wrist—and trace my finger over the screen.

Then I hear the most magical sound in the world. "It sounds like horses galloping," I tell her.

"Yep, babies' heartbeats are faster than ours, and your little one has a strong beat."

"Is it a boy or a girl?" I ask. Excitement filters through me for the first time since the doctor uttered the words 'you're pregnant' to me a few short hours ago.

"It's too soon to tell but going by these measurements, I'd say you're about six weeks along." I quickly count back in my head and deflate when I realize six weeks ago I was in New York. As much as I feared that was the case, hearing it confirmed shatters my heart and I begin to cry.

Hendrix isn't the father.

"Hey, it's going to be all right," the technician reassures me.

Shaking my head, I sniffle. "No, it won't because it's not his, it's …" I can't finish the sentence. Saying it out loud will make it official, and I don't want *him* to be the daddy. I want Hendrix to be the daddy.

The technician finishes up and tells me to call the doctor's office to make an appointment for four weeks. With pamphlets in hand, I'm discharged and I dishearteningly make my way back to school.

Of course, fate is a bitch and as I walk toward the exit, I look up and see the Lords standing just outside, and like a heat-seeking missile, I look for Hendrix, but I don't find him. I don't know if I'm relieved or sad but whatever the case, I can't hang around here all day.

Taking a deep breath, I head out and walk past them toward the waiting Uber I ordered. Remy calls out, but I'm in no mood to talk to anyone so I pick up my pace, but she reaches me just as I place my hand on the door handle.

"You okay?" she asks. Turning to face her, I see the moment it registers. "He knows about New York?"

Nodding, I swallow the lump in the back of my throat. "He knows," I quietly mumble, and I remember the look on his face when he realized what I'd done.

"Why do I get the feeling there's more?"

"'Cause you're observant but, Rem, I … I can't talk about this right now. I … I…"

She nods and takes my hand, squeezing. My eyes well with tears at her gesture and when she says, "I'm here if you need anything," the first tear falls.

Nodding, I tug my hand free and wipe my face. Pulling the door open, I climb into the car. The driver pulls away, and I rest my head on the window.

Again, I find myself rubbing my belly. I look down at my flat stomach and for a brief moment, I'm excited but when I look up and see Hendrix standing by his car, that hurt comes back. This baby should be his, but instead, look-alike Hendrix is the dad, and I have no way of contacting him. I'm eighteen and pregnant. I'm going to be a single mom because I'm a stupid girl who slept with the wrong person.

I may have failed me, but I will never fail this baby.

Never.

I've been sick for what feels like the tenth time today. Whoever called it morning sickness is a lying asshole. It hits at any time of day or night, and smells I used to love, coffee for example, now make me sick. Combine that with the pain from losing Hendrix and my life and head are in the toilet.

The next day at school I tried to talk to him. I tried to get him to see me, but he shut me out. He's been avoiding me like the plague, not that I blame him. We need to talk but I know I need to give him space.

For now, it's best if we steer clear of one another.

Maybe after some time to process and accept my betrayal, he'll speak to me again. I can't force Hendrix to be a part of my life, and as much as I love him—and yes, I do love him. It took me losing him to realize that I do—I know whatever we had is gone.

Placing a hand over my stomach, I know I will love this baby unconditionally, it's what a mother does. From the moment I saw the blob on the screen, I was in love, like the first time I saw Hendrix Vanderbelt. I was smitten with that first glance … but I ruined that.

Cupping water in my hands, I rinse my mouth out, feeling exhausted from all the vomiting. I've barely been eating, and I know it's wrong, but the mere thought of certain foods makes my stomach churn. I know the baby needs it and so do I, but I can't keep anything down, so why bother?

Exiting the girls' bathroom, I come face-to-face with none other than the man himself, Hendrix. He's leaning against the wall with his arms crossed, showcasing his biceps. *Is he waiting for me*? The door bangs closed, and he lifts his head at the sound, and when he spots me, he clenches his jaw. *Clearly NOT waiting for me then.*

"Don't," I murmur, "I'm not in the mood for your shit right now." Turning around, I begin to walk away from him.

"Don't what, Quinn?" he barks, gripping my arm tightly and spinning me to face him. The pain in his eyes breaks me. He's always been so strong and he's hurting because of me.

"Hendrix, please," I plead again, dropping my gaze to

the floor because it hurts to look at him. "I can't do this now," I mumble.

"Too fucking bad, Quinn. I want answers," he tells me, his fingers digging into my flesh harder. Then his voice drops. "I deserve answers."

Taking a deep breath, I lift my gaze to his and nod. He's right, he deserves to know everything.

"Who's the father, Quinn?" My mouth opens and closes, but I'm at a loss as to how to voice it.

"Stop, please," I cry.

"Quinn," he murmurs softly before a vibrating "Fuck," leaves his lips and echoes in the corridor. The sound makes me jump. "Just tell me," he growls. "Who's the fucking father?"

"I ... I don't know," I whisper.

"What do you mean?"

Taking a deep breath, I close my eyes. When I open them, I turn my gaze to a spot on the wall behind him. "When I was in New York—"

He interrupts, not letting me tell him what happened. "So, it's his, huh? New York guy?" His voice deepens as he leans in close to me, his breath fanning across my face.

I just stare at him and nod because I can't utter the words out loud. He begins to chuckle, but it turns into a sound that I've never heard before. He's losing control.

"For the record, he looked so much like you and in my drunken state, I thought he was you."

"Surely you would have known it wasn't me when he didn't rock your world like I do."

"Cocky much?" I throw at him, glad we are joking and kind of us again.

He steps into me. "Baby, it's not cocky when it's the truth. My cock is the best you've ever had. I have a right mind to go to New York and fucking kill him for touching what's mine." Before I have a chance to reply, he presses his lips to mine in a quick searing kiss. Before it goes any further, he breaks the connection, winks at me, and walks away, leaving me standing here. I wonder what's going through his head and start to think that maybe, just maybe, he'll be willing to do anything to keep what we have. Then fear seeps in because knowing Hendrix like I do, he's probably going to do something stupid so I turn around and head off to find the only person I know he may listen to.

Knocking on their door, I wait. "Well, well, well, look what we have here. Little Miss Quinn Ellis is at my door. It must be my lucky day," Saint, one of Hendrix's triplets, drawls.

Just like Hendrix, Saint, and Thatcher have that matching smirk, it's iconic to them, The Lords, as are good looks and huuuuge … egos.

"I need your help," I spit out, hating the very words coming from my mouth but I'm out of options.

Saint raises an eyebrow, then takes a step back, letting me in.

Taking in his room, I see it's the complete opposite of Hendrix's. There isn't anything out of place, not even a pair of underwear on the floor.

"What can I do for you, Quinn?" Saint says, leaning back against the door, crossing his arms just like his brother.

"Hendrix." It's one word but it's all I can manage right now.

Saint smiles before chuckling softly. "What did my brother do now?"

"Not him. Me." My eyes fall to his feet, hating myself

even more for saying this out loud. Lifting my head, I go to speak but he beats me.

"You fucked up?" Nodding, Saint's eyes go wide with confusion.

"I'm worried Hendrix is about to do something stupid or maybe attempt to at least," I mutter softly.

"Nah, not Hendrix. I think you have the wrong brother." Saint smirks. "If you'd said Thatcher, I'd agree and be worried. That one's a loose cannon … well, he was before he became pussy-whipped due to Remy. So, what's up, Quinn? Spill the deets and let Uncle Saint fix things." My eyes widen at his reference to Uncle because it should be true, this baby should be Hendrix's, not Hendrix lookalike's, therefore making Saint an uncle.

"I-I slept with someone in New York," I admit.

"Fuck," Saint mutters. "Does Hendrix know?" he says as a matter of fact.

"Kinda, sorta, not really he …" I stop, taking a deep breath. "I don't want to lose him, Saint, but I think I already have."

Saint takes his own deep breath. "Listen, Quinn, Hendrix is a wild card, always has been, but he's fiercely protective of the people he loves and he loves you, even if he hasn't admitted it to you or us. You are it for him, Quinn, regardless of what's happened." A tear slips free before I can stop it. "Go to him and tell him everything," he says. "He'll be angry, which is justifiable, but I know my brother, he's not an asshole." I eye him. "Well, okay, he is an asshole but give him a chance. He might just surprise you."

Exiting Saint's room, I know I need to see him now. Get it over and done with. As I walk toward his room, I dig deep to find the courage to tell Hendrix everything.

Lifting a hand, I knock on Hendrix's door, hoping he's there. The door swings open and before me stands a dripping-wet Hendrix with nothing on but a white towel sitting low on his hips. My eyes rake over his body and when I land on his face, I see that famous cocky grin.

"What do you want, Quinn?"

"I want to talk. I need to tell you the truth. All of it."

Stepping back, he lets me enter. My arm brushes his as I step past him and like always, my skin sizzles. Dropping my bag on the floor, I take a few steps and take a seat on his bed.

Leaning against the door with his arms crossed, Hendrix stands there waiting for me to explain, but it takes a few moments for my brain to compute because I'm gaga over him.

Shaking off the sexy thoughts I'm having, I take a deep breath and tell him everything, leaving nothing out.

By the time I'm finished, Hendrix is rubbing his hand over his head, trying his best to control the impending temper I know that's brewing inside him.

"I'm so sorry," I whisper. I'm trying to be strong but release a soft sob, unable to hold it all in. Lifting my head, through my tears, I whisper, "I love you, Hendrix. I can't lose you over this."

He stands there, silently staring at me. I can't read the expression on his face. After a few beats of silence, he pushes himself off the door and strides toward me. Reaching out, he cups my face in the palm of his hand and stares deep into my soul. My eyes close at his touch and I memorize what it feels like, just in case this is the last time he ever touches me, but he surprises me when he slides one of his hands down to my stomach. He gently caresses my belly and drops to his knees before me.

"I'll be here, Quinn, even though this baby isn't mine. I'll be there. Because I fucking love you too. Nothing will ever come between us. Nothing."

Sitting here in shock, I rapidly blink as I process his words. I know he's said he loved me before but it was just in the heat of passion. He didn't mean those three little words but this, this is different. Those three words seem more powerful now, and the love we have for one another is now stronger.

Covering his hand on my belly, I stare up at him. He pulls his hand free, and I mourn this loss but squeal in shock when he slides his hand behind my head and drags me toward him. He takes my lips in a possessive, dominating kiss.

He pulls back and rests his forehead against mine. "I'm not going anywhere, Quinn," he repeats, "I'm where I'm meant to be."

A smile appears on my face, and in this moment, I realize without a doubt, I'm completely and utterly in love with Hendrix Vanderbelt.

HENDRIX

"I'VE MISSED THIS," I mutter to Quinn. We're lying on my bed snuggling. Something the two of us used to do but when it became too much, we'd push each other away. Kind of like what I've been doing to her all week. I've been avoiding her because I'm hurt that she's pregnant … and it's not mine. And yes, I may have gone about it by being a complete cunt to her, but it's not every day you agree to be there for your kinda sorta not girlfriend when she's pregnant with another man's baby. And I mean it, I will be there for her, but I needed time to process. Now that I've removed my head from my ass, it's time to man up and be there for her like I vowed.

"Me too, but it's kinda my fault we haven't."

"Let's not place blame." I pause. "How about we forget this last week happened and we start fresh. Let's pretend you've just found out, and I'm the baby daddy."

"You are the baby daddy in every sense of the term."

"Too fucking right I am. DNA schmeNA." Reaching down, I place my fingers under her chin and tilt her head up to mine. "We're having a baby, Quinn." She nods and smiles, then her eyes well with tears. "Hey, why are you crying?"

"'Cause I'm so fucking happy right now."

"So you're crying?"

"They're happy tears. I was so fucking scared I'd lose you."

"Never," I tell her. "From the moment I saw you in freshmen year, you were mine."

"I felt the same way. The moment my eyes landed on you, Hendrix, I was yours. My heart beats for you and only for you." She rolls on top of me and presses her lips to mine. Her tongue seeks access to my mouth and I willingly open. It slips into mine, and they tangle together in an erotic dance. "Make love to me," she whispers.

"The bab—"

She cuts me off, "Will be fine. Sex when pregnant is fine. It's not like I can get knocked up again."

"If I could, I would, you know?"

"Huh?"

"If I could get you pregnant so it's my baby in your belly, I would."

"You really mean that, don't you?"

"Every fucking word. Now shh, my baby momma wants me to fuck her."

"Pretty sure I said make love but I'm down for fucking too. As long as your dick is in my vagina—"

"Or ass. Or mouth."

"You know I'm always down for a good ass or throat fucking, but right now, I want it slow. I want it sensual. I want you to feel how much you mean to me, Hendrix."

Nodding, I slowly peel her clothes off and she does the same to me. She lays back on my bed, her dark locks fanning out beneath her like a chocolate halo.

"You are a vision, Quinn Ellis. A fucking vision," I tell her. "You're actually glowing."

"You need your eyes checked, but you can do that after you make love to me."

"Yes, ma'am." I can't help but throw a ma'am at her. She hates being called ma'am, apparently it makes her feel old, but before she can argue with me, I cover her mouth with mine. Silencing her.

Our tongues slide together as I slip my hand down between her legs. My finger effortlessly slides through her wet slit. "You're soaked," I inform her.

"Mmmhmpf," she mumbles against my lips.

Inserting a finger into her soaked channel, I pump my digit in and out, in time with my tongue in her mouth. She moans, and when I add a second finger and hook it, hitting that magic spot, her body stiffens. Pulling away from her lips, I watch as her eyes close and she gives herself over to her orgasm.

Opening her eyes, she smiles a sated smile. "Make love to me now, Hendrix … please?"

Nodding, I flip us so I'm now on top of her, cocooning her underneath me. She widens her legs, and I wiggle around until the head of my cock nudges her entrance. With my eyes locked on hers, I push in. Repeating the motion, I pump my hips, thrusting back and forth until I'm fully seated in her.

She reaches down and squeezes my ass. "More," she demands.

Energetically, I pick up my pace and fuck her harder, faster, and deeper. Our bodies rocking in sync. My balls begin to tingle but I can't come until she does.

Leaning down, I press my lips to hers and continue to pump my hips. Her breathing changes and she lets out a squeal, letting me know she's coming. Pulling back again, I watch as she falls apart beneath me. Seeing her come sets off my release, and I come deep inside her.

Collapsing onto the bed next to her, she snuggles into my side and throws her leg over me. My release leaks out of her, dripping onto my leg but I don't care. That was perfect in every way and a little bit of cum isn't going to ruin that.

Pressing a kiss to her temple, I sigh in contentment.

She kisses my chest. "That was ..." But she doesn't finish her sentence, she's completely spent and words are just too much for her.

"Yep." I nod in agreement, kissing her head again. "I think that's my favorite way to fuck you now."

"I love any way you fuck me." She giggles, and I don't know if I should be pissed she's laughing after we just made love, but then she says, "Remember the first time we tried anal?" She snort-laughs at the memory, and I shudder.

"Ohh my God, I thought I'd broken you. That scream you let out was shrill and would have been heard on the space station."

"That scream I let out was letting everyone know I went to Nirvana and back. I swear I saw God that weekend, you sure know your way around an ass."

"Only yours, baby. Do you remember what happened when you asked me?"

"Yes," she snaps, playfully slapping my chest, "you got me a detention."

"I still maintain it was you. After all, it was you who asked for me to fuck your ass ... in English."

... *"I want you to fuck my ass this weekend," Quinn whispers into my ear as Mrs. Plunkett waffles on about the English language.*

My head snaps toward her. "And you decide to tell me that now? In English." She nods, and I shake my head.

"But—"

"No, no buts. Well, there will be this weekend."

"Why did you shake your head?"

"Because you shocked me, that's all. Who knew that queen bee Quinn Ellis was so fucking dirty."

"Ummm, you corrupted me. I was sweet and innocent until I met you."

"Bull fucking shit—"

"Are we interrupting something?" Mrs. Plunkett says from above us. I was so wrapped up in Quinn and thoughts of her ass that I didn't even hear or see her approach.

"All good, Mrs. Plunkett. I was just asking Hendrix if he understood the task you set."

"And, what did Mr. Vanderbelt say?"

"Mr. Vanderbelt," I say, referring to myself in the third person, "does understand the task at hand, but was hoping that

Quinn could help this weekend BUT," I emphasize that word, *"Quinn is already stuffed full this weekend."*

Looking over at Quinn, her mouth is wide open, I've shocked her.

"Well, Mr. Vanderbelt, Miss Ellis can help you in detention this afternoon."

"If I remember correctly," Quinn says, running her finger back and forth across my chest, "you fingered me and slipped your pinky into my ass in detention that afternoon."

"That I did, and then after dinner, I took your ass. We didn't wait till the weekend."

"Good times," she says, placing a kiss on my chest. Then she lifts her gaze to mine. "Maybe you should fuck my ass now, for sentimental reasons."

"Maybe I should," I reply. "And for the record, I will fuck your ass, mouth, cunt, or fist anytime you want me to."

"Duly noted," she says with a nod. "Now, grab the lube and fuck my ass."

If you'd asked me this morning how my day would end, never in a million infinity years, would I have thought Quinn and I would be a couple, officially, and that we are going to raise a baby that isn't mine together. And I definitely did not think I'd be fucking her ass after becoming a couple and agreeing to raise a baby, but here I am, sliding into her ass, happier and more content than I've ever been before.

QUINN

… a few weeks later

"UGH, I'M SO FAT," I complain as I pull my uniform on after sneaking into an empty classroom to fuck Hendrix during lunch. My libido has really ramped up this past week. I'm almost out of the first trimester which means it's time for us to come clean, but I'm worried about the ramifications. Hendrix is happy for everyone to believe he's the daddy. I don't want to lie, but at the same time, I don't want to look like a whore 'cause I can't get in touch with the real baby daddy. However, before we face the world's judgment, we need to come clean to my parents and his mom.

"You are not fat," Hendrix says, pulling me into his arms. Since he found out about the baby, he's been protective and touchy-feely and ohh so alpha. It's exactly how I pictured he'd be when I was pregnant, but in my dreams, he IS the baby daddy. "You are glowing and beautiful, and you're going to be the bestest mom to our lil' slugger."

"Hendrix," I blubber, literally blubber, "why are you so sweet? And why the fuck am I crying again?" I unwrap another Tootsie Roll and shove it into my mouth.

"Hormones are why and as for me being sweet, let's just keep that between the two of us. I have a reputation to maintain. It can't be getting out that I'm soft."

"Your secret is safe with me, but call our baby slugger again, and I'll stab you with a rusty fork."

"Well, what are we going to call it? It is so impersonal."

"I, umm, shit, do we have to name her now? It's hard enough deciding on a name-name, I can't be choosing a belly name too."

"So, stick with slugger and it's all good." I eye him. "Okay, fine, slugger is off the table. How about ... ummm, Cletus the fetus?"

"If I said no to slugger, what makes you think I will lovingly call her Cletus the fetus?"

"I was just messing with you." He pauses, and it's cute watching him think of a nickname for our baby. "I've got it, Tootsie."

"Tootsie," I repeat, nodding. "It's cute, I like it, and it pays homage to my craving for Tootsie Rolls right now."

"Right?"

Hendrix drops to his knees before me and covers my belly with his hand. "How do you like that, Tootsie?"

And as if she agrees, she kicks. His eyes widen as do mine. "Did …" he drifts off. Awe written all over his face.

"I think she did." I nod in agreement. "Do you like the name Tootsie?" I ask and again, a kick is felt. "I didn't think I'd feel this for a few more weeks.

"Shows that our lil' slugger"—I eye him—"sorry, habit," he apologizes, "but it shows he's strong. Just like his mom."

And once again the waterworks start.

After drying my tears and another quickie, Hendrix walks me to class where for the rest of the afternoon, Tootsie flutters about in my belly. Her being so active gives me hope tonight, with my parents, will go well.

Hendrix sighs for the fourth time since we got in the car. He hasn't uttered a word, but you can feel the tension emitting from him. "It's going to be fine," I tell him, earning myself a groan. "Come on, Hendrix, it won't be that bad." He snaps his head toward me, and I giggle slightly at the look on his face right now.

"You know your dad hates me, right? In fact, I'm pretty sure I'm the last person he wants around his precious little girl." He air quotes 'precious little girl.'

"You are confusing me with someone else. Jack and Diane Ellis don't give a flying fuck about me."

"Babe, you are the apple of your dad's eye. Don't try and deny it."

Nodding, I try to hold back my smile because I know he's right. My parents and I are close. I guess being an only child will do that to the dynamics in a family. I wasn't spoiled as such, but I never went without either. If I wanted it, I got it, after I worked my ass off for it. Things weren't just handed to me on a silver platter. "Okay, fine, they love me, but they want me to be happy and and you make me happy, therefore, they will be happy to make me happy." But even as I say that doubt filters in because my father despises the Vanderbelts, especially Mr. Vanderbelt … like many people in this town did. When he was murdered, I don't think there was anyone who was actually upset. I don't even think his sister was, and that's saying something when your own sister doesn't care you are dead.

Hendrix indicates, cuts across traffic, and pulls his car into the underground parking lot at Crestwood Central Apartments. He parks in a guest spot, but neither of us makes a move to get out.

"Hendrix?" I whisper his name like a question when the silence becomes too much.

"Yes, Quinn?"

"Please behave."

He snaps his head toward me trying to refute my request. We both know my parents love me but seeing him with me, it might cause tensions to rise and Hendrix is a Vanderbelt. They are known for flying off the handle, on occasion, and this is an occasion where he may soar if my dad loses it when I share my baby news.

"Fine," he growls. "I'll be on my best behavior, but if he starts being a cunt, I won't be held accountable for my actions." Case in point in my previous thought but before I can reply, he exits the car and comes around to my side. My door swings open and he offers me his hand.

Suddenly I'm nervous and just sit here and stare at his hand.

"You coming?" he says, snapping my attention to his. He smiles down at me in only the way Hendrix Vanderbelt can and those nerves dissipate. They vanish into thin air and I know with him by my side I can do this.

Placing my hand in his, he pulls me up and kisses me deeply. He slides his hand into my hair, fisting his fingers between the strands and gently tugging, causing my clit to throb. I moan into his mouth. He breaks the kiss and rests his forehead against mine. Both of us breathlessly panting. "You know, we could totally leave, they'd never even know we were here," he suggests.

Pulling back, I slap his arm and shove him out of the way. "We're doing this," I tell him, even if his suggestion is highly appealing. Lacing my fingers through his, he closes my door and we head toward the elevator. Stepping in, I press the button for the penthouse after scanning my keycard. Only those with a key can get up to our floor.

The doors open and Maggie, our long-time maid, is there to greet us with her signature bright smile. "Quinn, Sweetpea, you're home," she says, pulling me in for a hug. I squeeze her back and hug her tightly.

Hendrix clears his throat behind me, making me smile. Pulling back, Maggie rakes her gaze over Hendrix, and a wave of jealousy spears through me when I see her smile at him. "And who is this fine gentleman?" she asks, lifting an eyebrow.

Taking my place next to him, I slide my arm through his and place my hand on his arm in a 'he's mine, back off' kind of way before I introduce him. "This is Hendrix, my boyfriend."

Her eyes grow wide, and she begins to smile but

quickly schools her expression when from the hallway comes a deep, "He's not welcome in my house." Then my dad's standing before us, glaring at Hendrix. His gaze drops to my hand on Hendrix's arm and he growls. My father growls like a protective papa bear.

"Daddy," I state, just as Hendrix whispers loud enough for my dad to hear, "Told you so."

"No daughter of mine will be with a goddamn Vanderbelt," he barks. "Over my dead body."

I half expect Hendrix to say "happy to make that happen" but instead, he stands like a statue next to me and doesn't move a muscle. It's taking all his effort not to snap, and my heart swells when I realize the sacrifice he's making right now. Sliding my hand down his arm, I grip his clenched fist in my hand and somehow, I manage to slide it open, slip my hand into his, and squeeze it. Reassuring him I'm here and I've got his back, but he doesn't relax under my touch. In fact, his whole body becomes rigid as my fuming father stands before us in the foyer.

Daddy's eyes are locked on Hendrix's, and I know I need to do something to diffuse this situation, but before I can, Daddy says, "Quinn, you know I dislike his family, you're better off without him. Trust me."

Hendrix scoffs. "Like your fucking shit don't stink, old man," Hendrix snaps between clenched teeth.

They glare between each other and needing to do something, I step between them. Not sure what teeny tiny me could do but it does lighten the atmosphere, until Hendrix grips my hips in his hands and my dad notices. Once again, he growls, further igniting the situation.

"Please," I beg, staring up at my dad, but before I can plead my case, my mother joins us.

"Quinn, what a lovely surprise." She beams, pulling me in for a hug. "Hendrix," she says over my shoulder. Her tone not giving away how she feels, and I think maybe Mom can help win Dad over when I drop my pregnancy bomb.

"Mrs. Ellis," Hendrix says back in greeting, his tone much softer than when he addressed my dad.

"Why did you bring him here, Quinn?" my father demands. His tone is gruff and the look on his face is just as rough.

Since I don't see us getting any farther into the penthouse, I decide to just drop my bomb here in the foyer. It can't get any more tenuous, right? So I step back in front of Hendrix and just blurt out my news, "I'm pregnant."

Both my parents' faces pale while Maggie gasps. As my news lingers in the foyer air, my father's face turns from white to red. His eyes fill with anger, and his murderous eyes are locked on Hendrix.

"You fucking little shit," he sneers. Pushing me aside, he steps toward Hendrix and grips his shirt.

"Daddy, stop," I screech.

Hendrix chuckles and removes my father's hands from his shirt. Quicker than *The Flash*, I squeeze between them and place my hands on Daddy's chest. He looks down at me, and with my eyes, I plead for him to stop.

"You'll never be good enough for my daughter," Daddy spits at Hendrix.

Clenching his jaw, Hendrix does his best to keep his temper under wraps. "I know that, sir," Hendrix replies, surprising me at how calm his words are. "But I will be there for her every step of the way."

"We won't support this, Quinn," my father barks, turning his hateful glare toward me. His words hurt, and the look on his face softens a little when I feel a lone tear slide down my face.

"I'm sorry, Daddy," I blubber.

Dad shakes his head and I have never seen disappointment like that reflected at me before. The solemn look on his face hurts and I need to get out of here. Turning my back on my father, I grab Hendrix's hand and punch the call button.

Thankfully, the car was still there and the doors open immediately. I pull Hendrix in behind me and he follows without protest. As the doors begin to close, he reaches out, stopping it. He points his finger at my parents. "I'm stepping up because I love your daughter, sir. You need to accept we're together and that we are having a baby because I'm not going anywhere. Where Quinn and this baby go, I go." He steps back into the elevator and the doors close, blocking us from the disapproving stare of both my parents.

Staring blankly at the closed door, a smile tugs on my lips because Hendrix just admitted to me, in front of my parents, he loves me.

"What?" he asks, turning his head to gaze at me.

"You," I voice, "you told my parents you love me?"

"With every beat of my heart, Quinn Ellis," he says. "With every fucking beat."

We exit into the parking garage and walk silently over to his car. Like a gentleman, he opens my door, but before I climb in, he grabs my hand and gently tugs. Turning my attention to him, I look at the man who loves me.

"I'm sorry they acted that way," he tells me, his voice soft and full of hurt.

"I expected them to be upset, but I didn't expect Daddy to speak to you like that." I pause and then add, "Sorry."

"What are you sorry for?" He furrows his brows in confusion.

"Sorry to drag you into my mess."

"Quinn, there is no one else I would fake being the daddy for."

"You really mean that, don't you?"

"Yep, now get in. Let's go tell my mom the news."

"What if she hates me too?"

"Trust me, she'll be over the moon."

"Can we tell her another time?" I ask.

"Nope, let's do it. Besides, my mom will be happy."

"How can you be so sure?"

"Because since Dad died, she's become a new person and I just know it, she'll be over the moon with our news."

And Hendrix was right, Estelle squeals with excitement when we tell her. She wraps her arms around me tightly and then brings Hendrix into our circle. My eyes well with tears because this is how I wanted my parents to react, but instead, hurtful words were shared by my father, and my mother never said a word. Their reaction hurt. I was expecting anger but not like that. Maybe once the baby comes they'll change their minds.

Her eyes too, fill with tears as she takes us at arm's length looking over us. "I'm going to be a grandma," she tearfully whispers.

"Yeah, Mom," Hendrix says, "you're gonna be a grandma." He smiles down at me, pulling me into his side and kissing my temple.

Gazing up at him, I realize as long as I have Hendrix and his love, Tootsie and I will be fine.

HENDRIX

OF COURSE, I expected that reaction from her parents and I absolutely fucking hate they hurt her. Thankfully, I was right about mine. Mom took the news much better, she's over the moon to become a grandma.

After spending a few hours with her and her regaling Quinn with stories from my childhood, we say our good-byes and leave. Just before we leave, I go take a piss and I send an SOS text to everyone. We are going to share our news with them too, no more secrets, we are going to tell everyone about the baby.

As much as I just want to spend time with Quinn

alone, she needs to be around people right now. She's hurting, and I want to see her smile again because when Quinn smiles, everything is brighter in the world. Quinn is the best person I know, hell, probably even in this world. Sure, she comes across as kind of a bitch and at times a full-on raging bitch, but underneath it all is a kind soul. She'd do anything for those she loves, even give you the shirt off her back if you needed it.

She's been thrown some shit in her life so far, but from now on, I'm going to protect her from the shit thrown her way. And after she has Tootsie, I'm going to get her pregnant again and she will carry MY baby. I've loved seeing her stomach swell, even if at the moment it just looks like she ate too much. And her tits ... Oh. My. Fucking. God, they are massive. She's always had a nice rack but now, come to daddy.

My mind drifts to the other afternoon and what went down in the library...

... Sitting in the library, I look over at Quinn. She has a pen between her lips, and she's concentrating on the passage she's reading. And me? Well, I'm concentrating on her lips sucking that pen, wishing it was my dick she was sucking on. She leans forward to grab her highlighter, and I get an unobstructed view down her top. The soft mounds of her tits spill over the top of her bra, and now I'm picturing my dick sliding between them and her licking and sucking the tip as it slides through.

"Can I help you with something?" she purrs.

Lifting my gaze from her tits to her face, she has that glint in her eyes that suggests if I were to slide my hand under her skirt right now, her panties would be soaked.

"Just admiring the view and imagining ..."

"Imagining what?"

"Fucking your tits. Spilling my seed across your chest and face." Her eyes dilate and she bites her lip.

"How quickly can we get back to your room?"

"Two minutes, max."

"That's two too long. How about you meet me in the back stacks, and I make that happen. But when you're done, you have to go down on me 'cause my pussy is soaked right now, and I reckon with one swipe of your tongue, I'll come."

"Deal," I growl.

Pushing my chair back, I take her hand in mine, pull her up to her feet, and drag her into the back of the library. Spinning her around, I press her into the shelves and slam my lips to hers. My tongue pushes into her mouth, hers into mine. Our tongues thrash about, fighting for dominance. She pulls back and stares at me, breathing heavily from our make-out session. Lifting her hands, she pops open the buttons on her school blouse one by one. Then she flicks the front clasp on her bra, baring her tits to me.

"Fuck, Quinn," I whisper-growl, "your tits are fucking perfect."

And showing me just how perfect she is, she pushes her tits together and circles her nipples. The tips stiffen under her touch and she moans when she tugs on them. Dropping to her knees, she stares up at me and huskily demands, "Come here so I can get your dick out and we can make your tit-fucking fantasy come true."

Stepping to her, she makes quick work of freeing my dick. She licks her lips and sucks on the tip. Her lips wrap around the head, and she gently sucks and hums, the sensation is phenomenal.

Pulling back, she lies down and beckons me to her. Dropping to my knees, I straddle her stomach. "You ready?" I ask as I *begin to stroke my cock. She nods and I push forward. The tip is leaking precum and it's just the right amount of lubrication. I guide my dick to her chest, and she pushes her tits together again. My shaft slides between her soft mounds and it's heaven. Back and forth I thrust, this is better than I ever imagined and then she takes it to the next level when she lifts her head, opens her mouth, and licks the tip as I slide back through.*

With each thrust, I push deeper and deeper into her mouth.

"You look so fucking hot right now," I tell her.

"It's so fucking hot from this angle too, but I wish you were inside me."

Stretching my arm behind me, I continue to fuck her tits and contorting myself, I reach down between her thighs. Maneuvering her skirt out of the way, I slide my hand under her panties and my finger slides down her slit.

"Fuck, you're soaked," I tell her as I push a finger into her cunt.

"Yes," she yells.

"Shhhhh," I hiss, "we don't want to get caught."

We really should have gone back to my room, or hers, but seeing her like this will be worth any detention. My balls begin to tingle. "I'm close," I tell her.

"Mark me," she pants. "Mark me with your cum, Hendrix."

Pulling my shaft from her tits, I stroke myself twice and then come. Milky white jets of semen splatter across her tits and chin. She opens her mouth, and I aim the last of my release at her waiting tongue.

Quickly I spin around and lower my head to her cunt, licking and lapping at her as I continue to thrust my fingers in and out. When I bite down on her clit, she lets out a yelp and her body stiffens beneath me as she reaches her climax. I lick and suck until her body relaxes beneath me.

Rolling off her, I flop to my back, breathlessly panting.

Sitting up, I look down at Quinn, she's covered in my cum, and I can't help but smile. "Fuck, I wish I had my phone so I could take a photo of you covered in my cum."

"Next time," she replies. "But we need to get dressed before we get caught."

No sooner have we redressed and the librarian comes around the corner, a knowing look on her face but without proof, no detentions are given.

Quinn and I quickly return to our things, but I can no longer concentrate because all I can focus on is my dried cum on her chest.

"What are you grinning at?" she asks when I pull into my spot at school.

"Last week in the library." Her cheeks darken as she remembers too. "And you still owe me a picture," I tell her.

"Well, maybe after we tell everyone, we can do it again and snap a pic for you to jerk yourself off to."

"You are fucking perfect, Quinn Ellis. Now, let's go tell everyone you're pregnant, and then I'm going to fuck your titties and mark you."

"What's the SOS?" Saint asks as he walks into my room, the last one to arrive. He's becoming increasingly aloof these days, and I've noticed a change in him. I wish he'd open up to us and tell us what's wrong, but then again, he's a Vanderbelt and we are kind of assholes. Secrets is our middle name so we'll just have to wait for him to pull his head out of his ass and come to us when he's ready.

Looking around at everyone; Thatcher and Remy, Reign, Alani, and Hudson, Saint and Rowan, and our cousin, Rian—who is surprisingly sober right now—a smile graces my face. I realize I love each and every person in this room and I know Tootsie is going to be spoiled rotten by his aunties and uncles.

"I have news," I tell them. Then I take Quinn's hand and squeeze. One out of two reveals has been good. Can we make it two for three? "Well, we have news."

"You two get hitched?" Reign asks before he starts humming the "Wedding March," causing Quinn to giggle. It's nice to see, because all afternoon she's been in her head over her parents' reaction. I wanted to throat-punch her dad for the way he spoke, but I refrained because I knew doing that would only worsen the situation, confirming his thoughts about me. I will make this right between her parents, but first, we need to tell my brothers and our friends.

"No." I shake my head, but the thought of being married to Quinn and raising our baby together doesn't scare me. I make a mental note to revisit that idea at a later date.

"We're having a baby," I say, just as Quinn announces, "I'm pregnant."

"No fucking way," Thatcher mutters as he jumps up and hugs both Quinn and me. Everyone follows suit, and after everyone congratulates us on our announcement, the conversation turns to us and Tootsie.

"You know," Saint says, interrupting the girls and their chattering about baby things and stuff I don't want to know, *what the hell us a mucus plug?* "I thought Thatch and Rem would be the first."

"Hey," Remy scoffs, but Thatch looks at her in a 'really' kind of way.

"He's right, Peach."

Reign agrees, nodding. "You two do fuck like rabbits."

"Says the man fucking two people," Remy replies, crossing her arms and looking all butthurt but then she looks to Quinn and smiles. "So how did this happen?"

"Well, when a penis"—I poke my index finger out straight and make a hole with my thumb and forefinger on my other hand—"and a vagina hug—"

"Ohhh my God, Hendrix." Quinn laughs, smacking my arm. "She doesn't mean that." She looks so carefree right now, and this is how I wanted to see her when we told her parents. I wanted them to be excited like my mom and brothers are. Hopefully, once the shock wears off, they will come around but if I know Mr. and Mrs. Ellis, Hell will freeze over before that happens.

"But seriously, how did it happen?" Remy asks again.

"It just happened," Quinn says, and I see the look of fear in her eyes.

"When are you due?" Alani asks, taking the focus off the how and to the when, which seems to relieve her. Her shoulders relax and she smiles, the smile that could brighten the darkest of nights.

"I'm almost three months along."

"You're still so tiny," Remy says.

"And your tits are amazing," Saint says, earning himself a smack up the back of the head from me.

"Stop looking at her tits," I growl at him, seconds away from gouging his eyeballs out of his head and shoving them up his ass.

"Hey, I can appreciate a fine rack just like the rest of us, and Quinn has always had a nice set but now, hubba hubba." That eye gouging desire has been replaced with the need to murder my brother, but from the corner of my eye, I see Quinn blushing and looking bashful. She looks beautiful. Seeing her relaxed and carefree calms me.

"Thanks for the compliment, Saint, but if you want to keep breathing, I suggest you look at someone else's tits." She head nods to Rowan, who I will admit—in my head, never aloud—has a nice rack, "I can feel the anger radiating off your brother, and I can't afford to have him go to jail. Tootsie and I need him."

"Who the fuck is Tootsie?" Reign asks, furrowing his brow in confusion.

"The baby," I proudly say as I rest my hand on Quinn's belly. "It felt impersonal saying it, and we don't know if it's a boy or a girl, so Tootsie it is."

The rest of the afternoon and into the evening is spent hanging around in my room before we move to the cafeteria for dinner. Quinn and I walk hand in hand at the back of the group. Our hand-holding openly shows we're together and I wonder why we didn't do this sooner, so I ask her, "Quinn?"

"What's up?"

"Why did we never do this sooner?"

She furrows her brows in confusion. "Do what?"

"This." I lift our joined hands.

"Hold hands?"

Nodding, I wait for her reply. "'Cause you were you and I was me."

"That makes no sense," I tell her.

"We never made sense before, Hendrix." She pulls on

my hand, halting us. "Hell, I'm still not sure we do. I mean, you are only with me 'cause I made a mistake."

"No," I refute, shaking my head. "Get that thought out of your pretty little head. I'm here because I love you. The baby was the wake-up call I needed to see what was right in front of me because you and me, babe, we are meant to be."

"But Tootsie isn't yours," she whispers, her eyes welling with tears.

"Tootsie may not have my DNA, but I will be there for you and him. I can't explain it, but I just know you guys need me and I will be there. Day or night. You're stuck with me, Quinn Ellis, and one day, I'll slap a ring on your finger, and we will be together forever. Now, let's go. Daddy's hungry."

"Please never refer to yourself as daddy again, that's creepy as fuck."

"I don't think moms are meant to swear."

"Well, I'll stop swearing when you stop swearing."

"Fuck that," I tell her. "Fuck is one of the best words in the English language. Along with discombobulated and snickerdoodle."

"You are something else, Hendrix Vanderbelt, and this kid and me are lucky to have you."

QUINN

"YOU ARE SOMETHING ELSE, Hendrix Vanderbelt, and this kid and me are lucky to have you," I tell him, and I mean it. Laughter and joy fill my chest right now. Who knew I would find my happily ever after with Hendrix Vanderbelt? It's totally unconventional what's happening between us right now, but he and I have always been unconventional. This baby is what we needed to see what was right in front of us. My only regret is he isn't the actual father but like I just told him, Tootsie and I are lucky to have him on our team. If I was doing this on my own, I don't think I'd cope. Hendrix has been there for me, and I will never be able to thank him enough.

Before this, we were nothing more than fuck buddies and, at times, enemies. We would push each other away because we were too scared to admit what we really felt for one another. But the sex is ah-freakin-may-zing and we always gravitated back to one another, so I put up with his Lord's bullshit so I could have him. And since I've gotten pregnant, the amazingness has increased tenfold.

I'm humming along to myself, organizing a list of what I'll need for the baby, when a soft tap sounds at my door. Dropping the list on my bed, my feet pad across the floor as I head toward the door. Swinging it open, I'm surprised to see my father waiting on the other side.

"Daddy," I mutter as he bends down, kissing the top of my head. Without another word, he walks into my room and takes a seat on my bed.

"Quinn, princess, we need to talk," he tells me and I can tell from the tone of his voice it will be about Hendrix and the bomb we dropped yesterday.

"OOOOOkay," I draw the word out as I sit and take the spot next to him, crossing my legs crisscross applesauce style.

Patting my knee, Daddy gives me a soft smile. "I'll take care of everything if you get rid of the boy," he says as if getting rid of Hendrix means nothing.

"No, Daddy," I screech, stomping my foot as I stand.

"Quinn. " His voice rises. "Your—"

"Please, Daddy, can't demand for me to do that." Dropping to my knees before him, I look up and plead with my eyes. "I care about Hendrix a lot, and he cares about me. The baby too."

"He's a Vanderbelt, Quinn. He cares about himself and

that pretentious last name of his. He's a no-good, lying piece of shit who will leave you once this baby comes. He's not right for you, princess."

"You don't know Hendrix like I do," I cry, my tone not as tough as I want it to be because deep down, a part of me agrees with him. Hendrix and I are complicated, but when we're good, it's fucking amazing. Better than amazing, we are the literal definition of a couple who belong. But when we explode, it makes the aftermath of a hurricane look like a gentle breeze blew through.

Tears fill my eyes. My father can demand all he wants, but Hendrix is it for me and this baby because as volatile as we can be, I want him. He isn't like his father, he's amazing and I know we can do this. We can be a family and one day, I'll have his baby, and everything will be perfect.

A smile forms and my father sighs heavily because he knows I've made up my mind. After all, I get my stubbornness and tenacity from him. He runs his fingers through his hair and looks intently down at me. He gives me a sympathetic look, and I know he's going to try once again to sway my choice.

"Quinn, the Vanderbelts are all the same. They only care about themselves, and no matter what he tells you, no matter what he does, he won't stick around."

"Hendrix is different, Daddy, he loves me."

"Quinn." His tone says he thinks I'm making the wrong choice, but even with the doubts I have, I know what me and this baby need, and we need Hendrix but most of all, I want him.

"No," I refute, shaking my hand. "Hendrix is it for me." Holding my father's gaze, we enter into a stare-off until finally he looks away. He stands, pulling me into his arms and kissing the top of my head. I wrap my arms around my father's waist, and I know I've won, for now.

"Just be careful, Quinn. I can't lose you." Smiling into his chest, I know he means that and I'm going to show him he's wrong about Hendrix.

Pulling back, I smile up at him. He nods but there's something in his gaze. Before I can ask him, he turns away from me and exits my room without another word.

The door clicks closed behind him, leaving me alone. I stand here, staring at my door, wondering what my father knows. His warning is slightly unnerving, and it makes me think he isn't sharing something with me, but that can wait. I need Hendrix 'cause, well, pregnancy hormones, and well, he's Hendrix. My Hendrix.

Grabbing my phone, I text Hendrix telling him to come over. After an hour of not hearing from him, I text again, but again my text goes unanswered, and then Dad's words come back to haunt me. *They only care about themselves, and no matter what he tells you, no matter what he does, he won't stick around.* Is what he said true? Will Hendrix really just walk away?

Shaking away those thoughts, I decide to shower and freshen up for when Hendrix finally gets here. Grabbing my orange towel and toiletries, I open my door, and just as I close it behind me, a sudden sharp pain forces me to drop everything. My hands immediately grip my stomach and I hunch over, breathing deeply until the pain subsides. Once it's gone, I bend down and pick my things up but just as I straighten up, another searing pain tears through my abdomen, causing me to drop my things again. This one has me gasping out loud and tears filling my eyes. I bite my lip to hold back the cry of agony.

When it passes, I pick up my belongings again and

walk toward the bathroom. Rowan is doing her makeup when I walk in.

"Hey, girl," she says, applying some lip gloss.

"Hey," I reply, but my tone is soft and not like me at all.

"You okay?" She stops what she's doing and stares at me through the mirror.

I begin to nod, but another pain has me bending over, gripping my stomach and yelping like a banshee.

Rowan drops her gloss and rushes over to me. She rubs my back and waits tentatively as I compose myself. "I need the toilet," I tell her. Nodding, she helps me into one of the stalls, but I'm in so much pain that I just stand there. My eyes well with tears as she helps me pull my pants down—this is not weird because Rowan and I have experimented together before, but it's weird in the sense that anyone might walk in and the scene could be misconstrued. A soft whimper leaves me when my pants are midway down and I see blood in my underwear.

"Shit," Rowan mumbles. "Okay, let's get you up. I'm taking you to the hospital."

We're in Rowan's car and halfway to the hospital before I even realize I left my phone in my room.

"I need to let Hendrix know," I whisper, trying my best to hold back the tears, but I fail because they begin to fall down my cheeks.

Without taking her eyes off the road, she hands me her phone, and I scroll through her contacts. Of course, she doesn't have Hendrix's number, and I don't know his by heart so I text Saint, letting him know what's happening.

Dropping her phone, I rest my head on the window and hold my stomach. Praying Tootsie is going to be okay and Hendrix will come.

HENDRIX

"A WORD, MR. VANDERBELT." Mr. Ellis grunts, coming to a standstill at my side.

Saint and Reign stare at him with wide eyes. Having just heard what I'd just told them about his reaction to Quinn, me, and Tootsie, I was expecting anger or something. So I'm taken aback by both them and him, even if a part of me wants to tell him to shove a pineapple up his ass pointy end first, but the soon-to-be dad me, plasters a smile on my face and I smirk up at him. "By all means, Mr. Ellis." I stand up and lord my extra few inches over him. "But know, I'm only doing this for Quinn." I look at my brothers. "You mind giving me and Gramps here a moment?"

Without a word, they both rise, trying to hold back smirks and walk away, leaving me and Quinn's dad alone. Being a gentleman—when I need to be—I offer him one of the seats just vacated by Saint and Reign. He takes a seat, and I do the same.

"You wanted to chat?"

"You need to stay away from my daughter."

"Not happening." Who the fuck does he think he is? No one tells me what to do, much less him, and especially not after the way he spoke to Quinn earlier. No one speaks to her like that, not even her father. "Quinn and your grandbaby are my responsibility now. You lost that responsibility when you told her to get out after sharing the news."

"She's my daughter."

"And she's the mother of my unborn child. I will do whatever Quinn and Tootsie need."

"Tootsie?" he asks, confusion marring his face.

"Our baby, it felt impersonal to say it, or him, or her, and since Quinn can't stop eating them, Tootsie it is."

A smile appears on his face for a brief moment before he quickly schools it. "What will it take for you to walk away?"

"Nothing you can offer will make me walk away. I don't know what I've done to garner the hatred you have toward me—"

"You're a Vanderbelt. Do I need to say more?"

"I'm not my father, sir, just like I'm sure you're not like yours." From what Quinn has told me, Mr. Ellis Senior makes my dad look like a puppy dog. He was so crazy and unpredictable he was removed as a Lord. He's the only Lord to ever be stripped of his title, and a rule was made that no Ellis ever will become one. We will need to amend that rule if Tootsie is a boy because my son will be a Lord one day just like I am. It's an honor to be one, and it's an honor I will pass down to my son, blood or no blood.

"Words without action have no meaning," he throws back at me.

"And words have the power to hurt and you, sir, hurt your daughter." I pause and watch *my* words sink in. "Do I deserve Quinn? Fuck no, but she chose me, and I will choose her each and every-fucking-time. Your daughter is amazing, and she brings out the best in me. I cannot wait to see her become a mother, a mini-Quinn running around is just what the world needs. I will be by her side every step of the way. Whatever she wants, she will get it. If you want to be a part of her and this baby's life, you need to accept I'm a part of her life now too. Quinn and I are a package. End of fucking story."

He stares at me and processes my words. "You've surprised me, Hendrix, and you are right, we are nothing like our fathers, but you fuck over my daughter and grandchild and I will fucking kill you."

"I love them, sir. If I fuck them over, I will dig my own grave and hand you the gun."

"You love her?"

"With my whole fucking heart," I honestly tell him. "I told you the other day I do. It wasn't just a comment to piss you off. I love her with all my heart, sir. She hurts, I hurt. I love her," I whisper those last three words and smile. My mind drifts back to the moment I realized I loved her ...

. . .

… *"You are such a fucking asshole, Hendrix Vanderbelt."*

"And you, Quinn Ellis, are a fucking stuck-up bitch but for some fucking reason, I love you."

My words shock her and for the first time ever, I've stumped Quinn Ellis and she'd speechless. "You … you love me?"

Those three words flew out of my mouth before I could pull them back, but as I stare at a shocked Quinn, I realize I'm not freaking out.

I realize I do love her.

I

Love

Quinn

Fucking

Ellis.

"Of fucking course I do. I have since the ninth grade. You frustrate me to no end but, Quinn, you light up a room when you walk in. You make the darkest of days less dark. You know my deepest darkest secrets, and you give the best head I've ever had." She slaps my arm at that comment. "But seriously, Quinn, I do. I fucking love you as much as I hate you."

"They say love and hate coincide together, and with us, it's true 'cause I fucking hate you as much as I love you too."

Grabbing her cheeks in my palms, I slam my lips to hers and kiss her, letting my lips and tongue convey all my love.

The sound of Saint's panicked voice snaps me back from my memory. "It's Quinn. You need to get to the hospital."

"What?" I hiss, standing up and walking over to him.

"Quinn just texted me from Rowan's phone."

"What's happening?"

"Fuck if I know. The message just said she's on her way to hospital and to let you know."

"What else?" I growl at my brother, feeling helpless right now.

"Sorry, man, that's all I know."

Pulling my phone out, my eyes widen when I see several text messages from her. "Shit," I snarl, my phone was on silent, and I missed them. Quickly I bring up her contact and dial, but it just rings out. "Shit," I hiss again, "I can't reach her."

"I'll try Rowan," Saint says but his call rings out too.

"Fuck," I cry out, running my fingers through my hair. "What do I do?"

"Maybe go to the hospital," Reign offers.

"I'll drive," Mr. Ellis says. The sound of his voice startles me. I completely forgot he was here. As soon as I heard Quinn was heading to the hospital, my heart stopped and everything I was just doing faded out of my head.

Nodding at him, we silently make our way out to his car.

"She's going to be okay," he says as we reach his car.

"You don't know that," I snap back at him, my heart racing with worry.

"I do because my daughter is a fighter. Now get in."

He unlocks the car and we climb in. Mr. Ellis backs out of his space and floors it out of the parking lot.

Staring at my hands, I think about Quinn and Tootsie. My stomach is in knots that Quinn is alone and that something might be wrong with Tootsie. I only just got them officially, I can't lose them. I just can't.

QUINN

LYING ON THE HOSPITAL BED, I stare at the ceiling, my hand running back and forth over my stomach. Tears well in my eyes as every worst-case scenario plays out in my mind. I'm so scared I'm going to lose Tootsie and pissed off that Hendrix isn't here.

Maybe Dad was right after all?

The first sign of trouble and he's nowhere to be found. He's all talk, just like always. I've lost count of the times over the years he's let me down. Why did I think this would be any different? He's not even the father so do I have a right to be angry with him? Yes, I internally shout at myself. I do have a right to be pissed off because he promised to be here and he's not.

The first tear falls and I begin to sob.

Rolling to my side, I curl up into the fetal position and cry my little heart out. I'm pregnant and alone, just like my dad predicted. I don't know if I'm strong enough to do this by myself. I'm not Mary Poppins, I'm not good with kids and I can't sing for shit. How will I soothe Tootsie when she's upset? I remember my mom singing when I was upset and it always fixed it, or made me feel better when I was sick. Hell, I haven't even held a baby before. I'm going to be a shit mom and that thought causes me to cry harder.

The curtain to my room is pulled back, but everything is a blur from the tears pouring out of me. Wiping at them, my vision clears, and before me I see Hendrix and my dad.

Together.

I must be hallucinating because there's no way in Hell they would be here willingly at the same time.

My vision blurs again but when Hendrix growls, "Quinn, baby," I know I did see him. I'm not hallucinating. He stalks into the room and climbs onto the bed. He pulls me into his arms, and the warmth of his embrace causes the tears to commence again. Holding on to him tightly, I fall apart in his embrace. He whispers sweet nothings into my ear, reassuring me he's here and it's all going to be okay.

"Where were you?" I tearfully mumble into his chest. "You said you'd be there and when I needed you, you weren't." Pushing off his chest, I sit up. "I was all alone," I shout. "I needed you and you weren't there. You promised, asshole, you promised." Those last two words are muffled through my tears. I'm a sobbing mess now, and the machine I'm attached to begins to beep erratically, but no matter how much I try to calm down, I can't. I feel like I'm suffocating.

A nurse races into my room and demands that Hendrix "move." I have never seen someone move so quickly once he's out of the way. She pushes a button on the monitor to quiet it and focuses on me. She soothingly talks me down, helping me to get my breathing under control. The pressure on my chest eases and it becomes easier to breathe again. "That's it, sweetheart. Deep breath in and slowly let it out." We continue this for a minute or two, and then everything is back to normal. "Much better," she says, squeezing my hand. "Now, want to tell me what caused that?" She turns her gaze over her shoulder at my dad and Hendrix.

"It was a misunderstanding," Hendrix says before I get a chance to speak.

"It was no misunderstanding. You weren't there. End of story. You can leave now."

"Not happening, sweetheart," Hendrix throws back at me, crossing his arms defiantly. The movement causes his muscles to flex and my traitorous girly parts tingle as I take in his gorgeousness. I hate him, but I also love him.

"Quinn," Dad says, "give the guy a break. He's here now. That's all that matters."

"Why are you defending him? You hate him. Just like I do."

"You love me," Hendrix voices matter-of-factly. "Just like I love you and Tootsie. For the record, my phone was on silent. I didn't ignore you on purpose. As soon as I got your message from Saint, your dad drove me here. I was so scared. What happened?"

"You were with my dad?" I question, completely confused because the two of them hate one another with a fiery passion, but now I take them in, there's no angst radiating off either one of them. Dare I say it? They look chummy. Looking at the nurse, I furrow my brows. "Am I in a coma? I must be in some sort of dream."

"No, honey, no coma, but you need to not let that happen again, otherwise, you will be spending the rest of your pregnancy on bed rest." She fiddles with my IV and then leaves.

"What happened?" Hendrix asks when the silence in my room becomes deafening.

"I had cramps and there was blood—"

"Is Tootsie okay? Are you okay? Has the bleeding stopped? Are you still in pain? Tell me, Quinn, what's happening?" Hendrix rapidly fires the questions at me one after the other, not taking a breath between them.

"I'm fine. We're both fine now."

"Okay, you're fine, but what happened?"

"I had a subchorionic hemorrhage."

"A sub whatic?"

"A subchorionic hemorrhage is bleeding that happens when the placenta slightly detaches from the wall of the womb. Hence the bleeding and cramps."

"What happens now?" Hendrix asks, sitting back on the bed and taking my hand in his. This has really shaken him, and now I kinda feel bad for being bitchy Quinn when he first arrived.

"Bed rest for a few days, a couple of extra appointments with the OB, and no sex."

"Well, you're fucked then. You're a sex machine—"

"I'm still here," Dad says, interrupting Hendrix and causing me to blush.

"Ohh shit, fuck, sorry, sir."

"I kinda guessed you were doing it since, you know,

you're having a baby, but I don't need to hear about it." Hendrix and I both chuckle at Dad's response. Then he shocks me when he steps closer to the bed. He reaches out and squeezes my foot. "I'm glad you are okay, Quinnie. Is there anything your mother or I can do?"

"You can start by telling me why you two are buddy-buddy all of a sudden. The last time I saw you, you hated him as much as you hate the Patriots."

"Hendrix and I have come to an agreement."

"Which is?" I hesitantly ask.

"If I fuck you over, I have to dig my own grave and then hand him the gun," Hendrix tells me as if he's talking about the weather.

"Riiiiight," I draw the word out, not sure how to process all of that, but it'll have to wait because my doctor just walked back in and I'm hoping I can go home.

"Quinn, how are you feeling now?"

"Much better, Doctor. Can I go home now?"

"Not today I'm afraid. I want to keep you overnight for observation, but all going well, you can go home tomorrow."

"Can Hendrix observe me at home?" I ask her.

"And what medical school did he go to?" My eyes widen and I purse my lips as I think about how I can get out of here. "Exactly," she says. "Until the bleeding is under control, we need to keep an eye on you and your little—"

"Nooooo," Hendrix and I shout at the same time.

"We don't want to find out what Tootsie is," I quickly tell her. "We want it to be a surprise."

"Okay, I'll be sure to make a highlighted note in your file so there are no more slipups, but as I was saying, until the bleeding is under control and your cramps have subsided, you'll be here. You also need to prepare yourself for the possibility of bed rest for the rest of your pregnancy."

"I can't laze in bed for the next few months. I have school and a life."

"Quinn, you need to listen to the doctor and look after yourself and Tootsie," Hendrix says, sitting on the bed and taking my hand again. My fingers slide through his and I hold him tightly.

"He's right, Quinn," Dad interjects. "We never told you this, but your mother lost a baby before we had you because she didn't listen to the doctors. To this day, she still blames herself because she didn't listen."

I stare at my dad in shock. "I never knew that. Why didn't you guys tell me?"

"It's still painful for her to talk about. She holds so much guilt for losing it. When she got pregnant with you, she followed all the rules and walked around on eggshells to make sure you were safe."

Holy shit, I never knew any of this. What else have they kept from me?

"Do you have any other questions?" the doctor asks, interrupting our chat.

Looking at her, I shake my head. "Not at the moment."

"Good."

"I do," Hendrix interrupts and before she can reply, he asks his question. "What happens now? And how do I keep Quinn and Tootsie healthy?"

"Once I leave here, I'll arrange for Quinn to be admitted. She'll be taken to the maternity ward for observation and staff will be on hand should the pain and bleeding worsen."

"And then what?"

"I'll check on her in the morning, and if all is well, she can go home, but she'll need to rest for a few days and then come to see me. If nothing has progressed after that, she can return to her normal life, but she will need to take it easy. No marathons. No hiking and no sex."

Hendrix snickers at that and I glare at him. The asshole blows me a kiss and winks. He fucking winks, and that little eye movement has my body coming alive. Why is fate a bitch? I can't jump his bones and he's all winky-winky at me.

While I was ogling Hendrix and sulking over no sex, the doctor leaves, but no sooner has she walked out and a nurse returns.

Paperwork is signed.

Dad takes care of the insurance.

And I'm whisked up to the maternity ward for my unwanted sleepover.

Dad and Hendrix follow behind. The two of them whispering and no doubt conspiring to work out how to keep me in bed and following the rules. If sex was on the table, I'd happily stay in bed as long as Hendrix was with me, but with sex off the table, well, bed, I'll have to find other ways to keep myself occupied.

Dad stays until I'm settled and then he leaves, with the promise to visit tomorrow with Mom.

"Are you sure I'm not in a coma?" I ask Hendrix a few moments after Dad leaves.

"Why do you ask?" He pulls the chair beside my bed

closer and takes my hand in his, his thumb brushing the back of my hand in a soothing and sweet manner.

"This thing with my dad. It doesn't seem real."

"It's real, I promise."

"How can I be sure?" I ask him, hating myself for doubting this is real, but seriously, one minute everyone hates everyone and the next, it's all a big happy family. Don't get me wrong, I'm ecstatic. It's all great, but it still doesn't feel real.

Pushing himself up, he stares at me. "If you were in a coma, would you feel this?" He leans down, grips my cheeks in his hands, and covers my mouth with his. My eyes close and I give myself over to the kiss, the kiss that is turning me on with each lash of his tongue against mine. All too soon, he pulls back and rests his forehead against mine. "Do you believe me now?"

"I believe you're a clit tease," I tell him. He scrunches his brows in confusion. "We can't have sex, and you go ahead and kiss me like that."

"I can't help it that I'm a master kisser. Now, what can I get you?"

"An orgasm." I huff and cross my arms, pouting like a child.

"If you behave and follow doctor's orders, I will give you all the orgasms you could ever want and need but while we wait for that, what can I get you?"

"You being here is all I need right now, Hendrix. I'm sorry for thinking the worst about you before."

"It's okay, but I promise to make sure my phone is never on silent again. I was so fucking scared when I got that message from Saint."

"I'm sorry to scare you, but if it's any consolation, I was scared too. When that first cramp hit, I thought I was being torn apart from the inside out and then when I saw the blood, my heart sank."

"I'm so sorry I wasn't there, Quinn. I'll do better."

"To be honest, kinda glad you weren't 'cause you fixed things with my dad."

"Me too, but what I told him, it was true. I will never intentionally hurt you, Quinn. I know we have a volatile relationship but at the end of the day, I love you ... and this baby."

"I'm sorry that it isn't yours," I sadly tell him. Every time I think about it, I hate I ruined this moment for him and me.

"You don't need to apologize at all. It is what it is. All that matters is you are both okay, and I'm so fucking relieved you are."

"Me too, and I'm going to do everything the doctors say because I can't lose her ... or you."

"I'm not going anywhere," he says as he climbs onto the bed and pulls me into his arms. Snuggling into him, for the first time all day, I feel content because he's right, with him by my side, everything is going to be okay.

QUINN

FOR THE LAST TWO DAYS, Hendrix and I have laid low in my room and we haven't left my bed. Actually, now I think about it, I haven't left this room much at all. The only times I've left is too pee or shower. And even then, Hendrix carries me as he doesn't want me exerting myself. And when I shower, he does it for me. Do you know how hard it is to NOT jump his bones when his soapy hands slide all over my body?

It's odd to lie in bed together and not have sex. "Do you find it weird that we've been in bed together for almost forty-eight hours and we haven't had sex?"

"Now that you mention it, yeah, it is weird BUT we've had some pretty meaningful conversations."

And he's right. I found out that after school, he wants to become an architect. He's always been good at drawing but I never knew that was his career of choice. There was no shocking him when I said that I wanted to go to design school with Remy.

"Do you think we are drawn to one another because we both have creative career choices?" I ask him.

"Could be ... or it just could be you're addicted to me and my dick."

"Says the one addicted to my vagina."

"What can I say, I like what I like but for the record, you are more than just a place to stick my dick. Quinn, you are my first thought in the morning and my last thought at night. When we're apart, I constantly wonder what you are doing and without looking up, I know when you've entered the room."

"Hendrix," I cry but the moment is interrupted when Remy and Alani arrive with lunch. The two of them have brought us all our meals since I got home from the hospital, and Remy even offered to do all my homework for me but I declined that offer. I'm pregnant, not brain dead.

They stay for a while after I demolish lunch but when I yawn for the fifth time, Hendrix kicks them both out. Then we snuggle under the covers together, I rest my head on his chest and the thump thump of his heartbeat relaxes me. Drifting off to sleep, I wake sometime later with Hendrix by my side, whispering to Tootsie about superheroes and a show called *The Boys* they can watch when they are twenty as it's a superhero show for adults and not kids.

A smile appears on my face as I lie here and listen to

him. Sensing me looking at him, he looks up at me and smiles. "Question for the mommy-to-be, if you could have any superpower in the world, what would it be?" Hendrix asks me.

"Ohhh, umm, I don't know. I haven't ever really thought about it."

"Seriously?" he asks, shocked that I don't know. "I'd want super speed because it is easily one of the most powerful abilities. Not only could it help you in bad situations or help you get to a destination more quickly, but you would have the ability to time travel. And if you wanted to, you could alter and change time easily with this superpower."

A smile appears at my face at his response. He's put a lot of thought into it. "What's yours?" he asks again.

"I honestly have no clue, I mean, superhero movies aren't really my forte," I tell him with a shrug, "so….."

"But you watched all the Thor movies."

"Hello, Chris Hemsworth," I tell him.

"Of course, you watched it for the guy."

"Guys, plural."

"Who else were you perving on?"

"Tom Hiddleston. Idris Elba and, let's not forget, Natalie Portman.

"You think Natalie Portman is hot?"

"Yep, she's no Scarlett Johansson, but I'll totally turn lesbian for both of them."

"Can I watch?" he asks.

"Sure, why not, it's not like it's ever going to happen."

"Have you ever kissed a girl?" he questions.

"Yep," I tell him. "Have—"

"Whoa, whoa, back the truck up." He shuffles up into a

sitting position and stares at me in disbelief. "You've kissed a girl?" I nod. "Just kissed?"

"Only on the lips," I tell him, waggling my eyebrows and smiling as I remember when I experimented.

He nods, processing my words and then his eyes widen in shock when he realizes what I'm alluding to. "Pussy lips?" he shouts and I can't help but laugh.

"Yes, pussy and face lips," I confirm, and you'd think all of Hendrix's Christmases had come at once.

"Who and when? And are there photos?"

Again, I chuckle at him wanting specifics. I have no clue why guys are so fascinated about two girls getting it on. Personally, I don't care who gets it on. As long as they are happy and consenting, kiss away I say.

"Who doesn't matter. When, it was last year and, no, there are no photos."

"Come on, please tell me who?"

"Nope," I shake my head.

"You canNOT drop that bomb and not give me details. Two chicks together is fucking hot."—my point from earlier confirmed—"but seriously, babe, the thought of you going down on a chick is making me hard."

"Sucks to be you 'cause we can't have sex."

"We can't but you have a mouth and hands," he tells me, waggling his fingers and sticking his tongue into his cheek simulating a blow job.

"Let me get this straight, you won't let me walk to the bathroom or shower by myself, but you'd let me give you a blow job?"

"Yeah, because all you'd have to do is open your mouth, wraps your lips around my dick, and then let me do all the work."

"So generous of you but if I'm not getting any, you're not getting any."

"You know, you can always tell me who it was to make up for it?"

"I could but then I'd have to kill you, and I don't want to do that 'cause I kinda like you, Hendrix Vanderbelt."

"You love me," he throws back at me.

"That I do, now, let's watch a movie and if you're good, I'll let you cup my boob."

FYI, he isn't good cause he keeps trying to find out who I got it on with and made me miss half the movie, but I'm not too upset because the movie was shit and taunting him with my secret was priceless.

"I'm about to grab one of my Louboutins and gouge your eye out," I screech at Hendrix a week later.

"Baby, come on, we all know you have a shitty shot, and you'd miss and probably damage your precious shoe."

"Fuck you, Vanderbelt," I growl at him.

Bed rest and I do not mix. I just want to go outside and sit in the sun, but no, Mr. Overprotective Asshole here won't let me. He's taking the term 'bed rest' to literally mean 'bed rest.'

Resting my hands on my hips I glower at him, smacking my lips. Hendrix walks over to me, slides his hands around my waist, and pulls me into him. He leans down and kisses the tip of my nose. Pulling back, he smiles and skims his hands around to the front, caressing my belly. My belly has popped in the last few days, but that's what you get from lying in bed all day long eating Tootsie Rolls and chicken nuggets dipped in maple syrup —don't mock it till you've tried it … and don't mock a pregnant lady and her cravings either.

"You need to hop back into bed, Momma."

"Do not Momma me, Hendrix. I'm quite capable of standing up for a few moments."

"I agree, but you will not be wearing six-inch heels while doing so." I eyeball him again. "Please, Quinn, let me dote on you. It's what I'm here for."

"You're here to do food runs for me and give me glorious orgasms," I say, trying my best to look sexy, hoping he will give in, but right now, his dick is locked up tighter than Fort Knox.

"Oh really?" He smirks. I nod, biting my lip, hoping my seductive eyes will work. He chuckles and steps closer to me. My breathing intensifies and my vagina throbs. I need a good fucking because this is the longest I have gone without sex in a long time and I have an itch that really needs to be scratched.

Hendrix raises his hand, threads his fingers through my hair and gently tugs the strands. His mouth hovers over mine. Our breaths mingle together. "I'll certainly give you as many orgasms as you like, baby." *Yes*, I internally shout, fist pumping the air. "But until the doctor gives you the all clear, there will be no orgasms, BUT I will happily make out with you."

Before I can protest and tell him he's an asshole, he presses his lips to mine and kisses me deeply. Sliding his tongue into my mouth, I moan when his tongue slides over mine.

Hendrix halts when a knock on my door echoes through the room.

"I'm going to kill someone," I growl, dropping to the edge of my bed while he moves to let the kissblocker in.

Throwing the door open, Reign waits on the other side, leaning against the jamb.

"This better be fucking good," I shout out.

Reign chuckles and then schools it and says, "It's Rian."

Even with his back to me, I know Hendrix will be worried. He looks back at me over his shoulder, and I was right, panic is written over his face.

"Go. Rian needs you," I tell him, but he hesitates. "I'll be fine," I tack on.

"Do not leave this room, Quinn." I roll my eyes at his bossiness. "I mean it, and I will know if you do."

"What are you gonna do about it?"

"No sex when you get the all clear."

"My eyes widen and my mouth drops open in shock. "You wouldn't?"

"Try me."

"Fine," I huff, dropping down onto the bed.

Hendrix lingers for a moment, unsure whether he should go or stay, but I'm fine. Clearly Rian isn't.

"Go," I demand. He nods but before he leaves, he rushes back to me and kisses me hard. Breaking the kiss, he grabs my hand in his and squeezes. With another quick peck on my lips, he follows Reign to go help his cousin.

Without Hendrix hovering over me, I flop back onto my mattress and decide to binge *Shameless* and eat my way into a nap when my phone beeps with a text from Rowan.

ROWAN

I'm coming to hang. Saint has left me to deal with Rian.

QUINN

Hendrix too, come join me, I'm watching Shameless.

ROWAN

Ooh Ian. I'm on my way.

I chuckle, seeing her response. That girl loves her some Ian Gallagher and me too, just don't tell Hendrix.

While I wait, I think about the earlier conversation with Hendrix about kissing a girl and my mind drifts back to the night when I experimented…

…Rowan has just moved into the room next to mine. It's so good that she's finally boarding here. Her dad, Mr. Ashford, finally relented and she seems much more relaxed now. We are in her room lying on her bed, our feet against the wall playing 'never have I ever' and passing a bottle of vodka back and forth. We are both pretty tipsy by this point.

"Have you ever kissed a girl?" I ask Rowan. She turns her head toward me and nods. "Who and when? And are there photos?"

"It was junior year and a Saturday night, I was staying here at school in Stacey Macdonald's room 'cause Dad was away at some school conference thing and, apparently, I couldn't be trusted at home by myself. She and I snuck out of the dorms and headed up to the cliffs. We sat on the old bench up there and just stared out at the ocean. A breeze picked up and 'cause we were only in our pajamas, we huddled close together for warmth. One thing led to another and we kissed."

"Holy shit," I tell her. "What was it like?"

"Kissing a girl is different than kissing a boy. It's softer. Sweeter. I kinda liked it," she says.

"Wonder if I'll ever get the opportunity to kiss a girl?" I whisper, more to myself than to Rowan.

"Quinn," she whispers my name and I turn my head to look at her. She's right there, our lips are millimeters apart. She leans forward and presses her lips to mine. My eyes widen in shock and my mouth opens. She slips her tongue into my mouth and I find myself sucking it in farther. She somehow coaxes mine into her mouth and then we are kissing. Rolling to our sides, I pull her closer and keep kissing her.

I don't know how long we kiss but when we pull apart, both of us are breathless.

"Wow," I mutter, rolling to my back. Once again staring up at the ceiling, but this time my lips are tingling, my heart is racing, and my pussy is throbbing.

"I hope I didn't cross a line," she says, her tone subdued. It sounds like she regrets kissing me.

Turning to face her, I shake my head. "Not at all." Then I quickly add, "That was one of the hottest kisses I've ever had, and my first kiss was with Hendrix Vanderbelt and that boy knows how to kiss … and I'm not just referring to the lips on my face."

"Have you ever, you know…" she asks.

"Have I ever you know what?"

"Kissed a girl down there."

"Considering I just had my first girl kiss, what do you think?"

"Ohhh yeah," she sheepishly replies with a laugh.

"Have you?" I ask her.

"Nope … but I've always wanted to."

Silence befalls us and I think about what she just said and

with my pussy throbbing from that kiss, I'm now intrigued to see what kissing a girls lips down there would be like. "Me too," I honestly tell her.

She's silent and now I wonder if I've made her uncomfortable. Sitting up, I cross my legs, crisscross applesauce style and stare down at Rowan, she has a contemplative look on her face so I just go for it. "Do ... do you want to?"

"Want to what?" she asks. Sitting up, she crosses her legs like mine and stares intently at me.

"Want to kiss each other down there?"

She stares at me for a few beats and then she shyly nods her head and whispers, "Do you?"

Before I know what I'm doing, I'm nodding my head and pulling my pajama bottoms off.

That was my first, and only, experience with a girl but I can unequivocally say, I'm not a lesbian. Girls kiss too softly, I like it hard and rough. I like how Hendrix kisses me, it's the perfect mix of sensual and dominate.

My trip down memory lane is interrupted when Rowan walks into my room and just like that night, we lie on my bed together but rather than making out, we watch *Shameless* and I gorge on Tootsie Rolls.

Rowan leaves just before midnight, after I yawn for the millionth time. Hanging with her was just what I needed and now, I'm feeling lighter and relaxed. A smile appears on my face because I really enjoyed my impromptu girls' night. It wasn't freedom, but it was something different. And at least Hendrix wasn't hovering over me and treating me like I'm glass. Like I'll shatter if the wind blows too hard. Don't get me wrong, I've become accustomed to him showering me with affection and treating me like a queen, but a girl needs space. And then I start to feel like a bitch that I'm whining over him hovering and not being able to have sex when our friend, his cousin, is in a downward spiral. I hope he and the boys can deal with Rian quickly because I miss Hendrix. And maybe, just maybe, we can pick up where we left off, and he can use that magical tongue of his on me … between my thighs. In this moment, I decide oral isn't sex so that'll be fine, right?

HENDRIX

"WHAT'S HAPPENED?" I ask as we all climb into Saint's car. Saint is in the driver's seat, Thatch is shotgun, and Reign and I are in the back since we were the last to arrive.

"Sorry for bothering you," Reign says from next to me, "but we need to stage an intervention."

"What did the asshole do now?" Our cousin has been spiraling ever since we discovered he was adopted and has a twin sister out there somewhere. Just another 'fuck you' from Dad from beyond the grave. We always knew he was a cunt, but the things we keep discovering make cunt seem not a strong enough word to describe him. Lucifer isn't even a description to use because he makes the king of Hell look like Tinker-fucking-bell.

"He turned up drunk at home, demanding Mom tell him who his real parents are, and no matter how many times Mom said she didn't know, he kept pressing her."

"Did he hurt her?"

"No, she managed to lock him in the laundry room, and that's when she called us."

"Good," I state, nodding my head. Then I run my hands through my hair in frustration. "This is really eating him up," I voice, hating this is happening to our cousin. "How do we help him?"

With my question out in the air, for the rest of the trip, we discuss options on how to deal with our out-of-control cousin, but when we pull up at Mom's, we're still at a loss as to what to do with our dear cousin.

Saint has just killed the engine, and we're all about to climb out when I look up at the home we grew up in, and see Rian stumbling down the stairs, a half-empty bottle of liquor in his hand.

"I thought he was in the laundry?"

"Mom said he was," Reign reconfirms.

"Fucker probably busted the door down," Thatcher says just as Rian begins shouting at us.

Sighing, we all exit the car, bracing ourselves to deal with a drunk and out-of-control Rian.

"I deserve to fucking know," he slurs before taking another huge gulp. He stumbles with each step, tripping over his own feet to get to us. "She sent you to spew more fucking lies, did she?" he snarls at us and lifts the bottle to his lips again, but Thatcher snatches it from his clutches before he can pour more liquor down his throat.

"Enough," Thatch growls, shoving him down so his ass hits the driveway below. "Getting shitfaced and yelling at Mom won't get you answers."

"Fuck you," Rian snaps. His eyes glaze over, and he lowers his head, resting his forehead on his knees. He starts tugging on his hair, mumbling incoherently to himself.

"Come on, man." I squat in front of him, tapping his knee. He lifts his head and looks up. He looks higher and his gaze flicks between the four of us. His eyes are glossy and not just from the alcohol. "Ri, come on, man, let's get you up and inside," I say, reaching for his armpit to help him up, but the stubborn asshole—he really is a Vanderbelt, blood or no blood—shoves me away.

"I can fucking do it," he snaps and pushes himself up into a standing position. He rocks side to side. Once he has his balance—ish—he pushes his way between us toward the front entrance, mumbling to himself while he staggers up the front stairs. The five of us follow and when we walk inside, we make our way to the living room.

Rian flops down ungracefully on the sofa and drops his head back, staring at the ornate ceiling above. My brothers take the other sofas, and I sit on the coffee table in front of Rian.

"You need to knock this off, Ri," Thatcher hisses. "Getting drunk every night won't solve your problems."

"It helps me forget," Rian confesses. He lifts his head and his gaze flicks between us as he explains how he feels. "Do you know what it's like to realize your life has been a lie? That your parents aren't your parents and you have a twin sister out there somewhere?" Once done, he lowers his head. His shoulders begin to rise and fall as if he's crying.

"Look, man," I say, placing my hand on his knee, squeezing to get his attention. He lifts his head and stares at me. Tears streak down his cheeks, and I hate seeing my cousin so broken. "Yes, it's fucked up. We all know that, but we'll help you figure it out. It's what family does."

"But I'm not family. I'm just some poor kid who was separated from his sister and adopted."

"Blood doesn't mean shit," I snap at him. "You are our cousin, and your mom and dad are your parents."

"Whatever," he sasses.

Our mother watches on from the entrance to the room, worry etched on her face, but she comes into the room and sits next to me on the coffee table. She reaches out and takes Rian's hand in hers. "Rian, Tamsyn and Michael love you unconditionally, and if you'd speak to them instead of giving them the cold shoulder, you will get their side of the story. They too are hurt by what Thornton did, but they never stopped loving you. They've always loved you, sweetheart. From the moment they brought you home, you were their son, and you still are. Even if you are acting like a spoiled brat right now." She pauses. "Would you like me to get them here and we can all talk about it?"

Rian stares at Mom, processing her words and then nods. It was only a slight movement of his head but with that one action, I see a sliver of the guy he was before his world imploded and everything bubbled to the surface.

"Thanks, Mom," I tell her, giving her a reassuring smile. She rises and leaves to call Tamsyn and Michael.

Silence fills the room until Rian farts. His mouth lifts into a grin, and then he bursts out laughing 'cause no matter how old you are, farts are funny. Once the laughter subsides, silence returns. That is until there's a knock at the front door and we hear Mom with our aunt and uncle.

"You ready for this?" I ask him.

"Nope," he honestly replies.

"Just talk to them calmly, but know we've got your back."

Mom, Aunt Tamsyn, and Uncle Michael enter, tension filling the room with each step they take. Rian turns his head, looking over at them. They look just as broken as he is. Rian stands and walks over to his parents. The three of them embrace, and all of us smile watching them as they hug and whisper among themselves. They are a family, and I think this moment reaffirms that for Rian.

If Dad wasn't dead, I think I'd kill him. He fucked over so many people when he was alive, but seeing my cousin and his parents now, I have a feeling that after tonight, we will have our cousin back and a plan to find his missing sister.

BY THE TIME my parents arrive, I've sobered up, a little. My eyes still have a whiskey fog to them, but for the most part, I can see straight again. When my parents enter the room, they both walk straight over to me and I to them. After we embrace, we return to the sofas. Hendrix gets up from the coffee table and sits on the arm of my chair. Mom sits next to me, and Dad sits where Hendrix was moments ago.

"Rian," Mom says, and the mellow tone of her voice cuts me. "I hate you're pushing us away, but that aside, I hate seeing you self-destruct. We nev—"

"Mom, stop," I interrupt her and shake my head, "you have nothing to apologize for. It's me who needs to beg for forgiveness. You and Dad have given me an amazing life. I just wish you'd told me. I wish we didn't have secrets."

"I know, and I'm sorry. I ... I couldn't have kids, and neither could your father. I so desperately wanted to be a mother, and watching Estelle have her triplets was so hard. Then she got pregnant with Reign, and I fell apart. Why did she get to have a family and not me? I hated feeling like that, but when you want something so much and it can't happen, it's hard. Then one day, Thornton came to me and said he could get me a baby. I jumped at the chance to finally have what I always wanted. I didn't ask questions, I just wanted to be a mom, and the moment you were placed in my arms, I was in love. If I had known you had a twin, we would have taken her too."

"You would have?" I ask.

She nods. "In a heartbeat."

"Rian," Dad says, "when we discovered you had a twin, your mom and I started looking for her. It's still early days, but we will not stop until we find her."

"What can I do to help?" I ask them, hope filling my voice.

"For starters, you need to stop self-destructing. No more binge drinking and no more accosting your aunt, who doesn't know anything."

Looking over at Aunt Estelle, I smile at her. "I'm sorry for earlier."

"It's fine, Rian. You're hurting and you needed an outlet. No one got hurt and now, now it's all out in the open and there's a plan in place. We just have to wait for the investigator to do his thing and then one day, you will be reunited with your sister. But just know, we all love you, Rian."

"I'm so lucky to have you all. I've been such a cunt—"

"Rian," Mom admonishes me, "language."

"Sorry, Mom. Let me try that again. I've been such a fucking asshole—"

"Better, but still," Mom says with a shake of her head and an eye roll.

"I was a douche," I say this time, earning myself a smile and nod from my mom at my new choice of word to describe myself, but to be honest, all three suit me and my actions of late. "And deep down I was worried I'd be sent away because I'm not a Vanderbelt by blood."

"Rian, no," Mom tearfully says. Reaching over, she takes my hand in hers and squeezes. "You are a Vanderbelt, one million percent. Blood does not make a family. I never want to hear you say that ever again. You are Rian Reginald Vanderbelt," Saint snickers at my middle name, but like he can talk, his are Clarence Benedict, "and you are a part of this family."

"Thanks, Mom." I raise my head and glance around at everyone. "I'm sorry for being ..."

"A cunt," Thatcher says, earning himself a slap up the side of his head from Mom. "Well, he was," he pleads, crossing his arms. "But, Ri, we've got your back and we'll be here, every step of the way."

And I need them because when it all comes to a head, no one is prepared for what we discover about my birth parents.

HENDRIX

QUINN IS GOING to kill me.

This thing with Rian took way longer than I antici-
pated, and I haven't called or texted Quinn once, but on a
positive note, I think we got through to him. Now with
Aunt Tamsyn and Uncle Michael on board, things will
hopefully start to look up for Rian.

Parking my car, I sneak up to the girls' floor and into
Quinn's room. I stop and smile when I see her. She's sound
asleep, snoring softly with her hand resting protectively on
her stomach. Her nightgown has bunched up around her
waist, and I notice she isn't wearing any panties. She rolls

to her side and one of her tits pops out the top of her nightie. My dick hardens in my pants, and if she wasn't on a sex ban due to the bleeding thing the other week, I'd climb onto the bed and slip inside her, but I will not risk our baby for a quick fuck.

Kicking off my shoes and stripping off my shirt and jeans, I climb into bed next to her in my boxer briefs.

"Hendrix," she sleepily mumbles, "what time is it?"

"Shhh, it's late. Sleep." Pressing a kiss to her temple, I watch her close her eyes again and mumble a "Mmmmhmpf," before she rolls onto her side, making me the big spoon as she snuggles into me. Her delectable ass rubs against my dick, she swivels her hips and I know she's awake.

"Quinn," I warn, but it falls on deaf ears. She reaches back between us and grips my dick in her palm. "You know we can't."

"I know we can't have sex but, Hendrix, I need a release and so do you."

"What are you proposing?"

"We both have mouths and fingers and you, sir, have a tongue that is amazing."

"Are you proposing a sixty-nine?"

"Call it what you want. I just need an orgasm."

"I don't want you exerting yourself."

"Sucking your dick will not exert me. Now, do you want this or not?"

"What sane man would turn that down?"

"Seems like you are," she snaps, and before she can whine again, I roll her to her back, spin around, and shove my face between her thighs. I lick her slit like it's an ice cream cone and when she moans my name, I thrust my tongue inside her.

"Yes," she mewls.

"More, please," she begs, grinding her pussy into my face.

Taking her clit into my mouth, I suck and kiss the little bundle of nerves. She cries out my name as I continue to kiss her.

"Fingers," she growls.

"I'll insert a finger when you return the favor," I tell her and then feel her fingers at the waistband of my briefs. She pulls them down, freeing my cock and balls. She licks down the side of my shaft, and I shit you not, I nearly come there and then when she sucks me into her mouth. Quinn can run her mouth at the best of times, but when it's full of my dick, it's just how I like it. All that flapping does something to the muscles in her cheeks, making her the best head giver in all the lands.

Together we pleasure each other with our mouths and fingers. Bringing the other to the edge and then stopping, drawing out the moment.

"Please," she begs against my shaft just as I was about to concede, but I'm glad she gave in first.

"Together," I growl.

"Together," she agrees and a few seconds later, the two of us bring each other to the brink, and this time, we don't stop. We suck, lick, and finger/pump each other until we can't see straight. Each of us plunging headfirst into our orgasm. Neither of us letting up until we've pulled every last drop out of the other.

Rolling off her, I stare up at the ceiling breathing heavily. She reaches out and takes my hand in hers, lacing our fingers together. We lie here and catch our breaths.

"Thank you," she whispers, breaking the silence.

"Why are you thanking me?"

"Because you gave me an orgasm."

"You never have to thank me for that. Anytime you need one, I'm here." Then I quickly add on, "As long as it's safe."

"You're going to be a good dad," she says, causing me to smile and then she sniffles. "I wish you were the real dad." She begins to cry and I hate it.

Sitting up, I pull her into my arms. "Quinn, baby, I am this baby's dad. As I said to Rian earlier tonight, blood doesn't mean shit. I'm Tootsie's dad, end of fucking story."

"You really are amazing," she tells me with a half-smile.

"I know," I cheekily reply. "Now let's get some sleep, we have English first up and Mrs. Plunkett is in a mood at the moment."

QUINN

… two weeks later

"IT LOOKS like the subchorionic hemorrhage has resolved itself," the doctor tells me, and I smile brightly. "Everything with this scan is looking good and as you heard, Tootsie's heartbeat is strong." I smile that she's also referring to the baby as Tootsie. "I'm happy for you to resume all normal duties."

Thank fuck for that. I was going stir-crazy being confined to my bed, and I was really getting pissed off with Florence Nightingale next to me here hovering day and night. Don't get me wrong, I loved having him around and lazing in bed together, but I couldn't even use the bathroom without him sticking to me like glue. I lost count of the number of times that he had to 'just check' my panties for blood and not once did he accidentally finger me while checking, except for that one night when he got back from the Rian emergency. Each time I wanted a release I begged like a wanton whore, but each time he refused for fear of hurting Tootsie or causing the bleeding to start again.

"Does that mean sex?" I ask her. From the corner of my eye, I see Hendrix shake his head, but I also notice he has a look of apprehension on his face. He's missing sex just as much as I am. Pregnancy sex is something else. It's like those extra hormones in my body are filled with kerosene, and one look or touch from Hendrix sets me ablaze and I need to be fucked. These pregnancy hormones are making me a randy teenage boy. They are making me turn into Hendrix.

She laughs and then pauses, I feel like she's going to tell me no sex for the rest of my pregnancy, and then she finally gives her answer. "You may, but nothing adventurous."

"Damn, Quinn," Hendrix voices. "No orgies on the cliffs for us until after Tootsie arrives."

"Hendrix," I admonish him, smacking him in the arm. "He was joking," I quickly tell the doctor. "We don't do that." It's bad enough I'm eighteen, a senior, and pregnant, I don't need her thinking we're sex freaks too.

"Hey, each to their own," she tells us with a smirk, reaffirming to me why I want her to deliver my baby. "Just be safe and take it easy."

"Thank you," I tell her as she wipes my belly. "I'll see you in four weeks but as always, if you start to bleed or anything else pops up, come and see me." With that, she shuts down the ultrasound machine and leaves me to get dressed.

I've just pulled my school uniform back on and when I look up, Hendrix is staring at me. There's a heated look in his eyes, and if we weren't in the doctor's office right now, I'd strip us both naked and ride him like a cowboy.

"What?" I ask him.

"You look so beautiful right now."

"Well, you look pretty handsome too."

"Wanna blow off the rest of the day and let me pamper you?"

Smiling at him, I walk toward him and drape my arms over his shoulders. He slides his hands around to my lower back, holding me to him. "I would love nothing more than to blow … the day off with you, and if you play your cards right, I'll blow you later too." I wink at him and grin like a carnival clown because I'm happy right now. So flipping happy. Tootsie is healthy, as am I. Mom and Dad are excited to be grandparents, finally, but most of all, Hendrix is here. He's by my side and excited for this baby. I wish with everything I had he was the baby daddy, that's my biggest regret in life, but at the same time, I wouldn't be pregnant with Tootsie if I didn't fuck up. It's one of those catch-twenty-two scenarios.

"Babe, most days end with that, but today, I think we should end with me sliding into your sweet, sweet cunt because it's been far too long since that's happened."

"Why not both?" I offer as an alternative.

"Did you just taco ad me?"

"Unintentionally, yes. But now, I want tacos, then I want to blow you, and then you can fuck me."

"I think that can be arranged. Now let's go."

"Holy shit, I'm full," I tell Hendrix, leaning back in my chair and resting my hand on my stomach.

"I'm not surprised, you just demolished twelve tacos. This kid is going to come out Mexican if you keep eating like that."

"Shut up, asshole," I mumble as I shove taco number thirteen into my mouth. I hold up my finger to halt what he is about to say, and when I've almost finished, I tell him, "You try growing another human being, this shit is hard. I'm always hungry. I have cankles. I need to pee six billion times a day and horny, fuck me sideways, I have never been so horny in my life."

That last statement garners the attention of the young guy at the table next to us. He gives me an 'I volunteer as tribute' look, and I shake my head at him. Sure, he's cute, but he's not Hendrix, and his is the only dick I want to ride right now.

"Well, as soon as you stop stuffing your face, let's get out of here and I can help you scratch that itch."

"You're so good to me," I tell him, my insides begin to buzz with what's to come—pun totally intended.

"Yes, I'm so good 'cause I wanna fuck you."

"Keep that nonchalant attitude up and I'll take ol matey behind you up on his offer.

"And ol matey there will be dead before he can even get his dick out. You are mine, Quinn Ellis. Your cunt is mine. That baby is mine. You got it? All-fucking-mine."

"Such a caveman," I tease. "Now, let's get out of here. Momma needs to be fucked."

HENDRIX

HAVE you ever tried to drive with a rock-hard dick while your girlfriend fingers herself in the front seat of your car? It's hard—pun intended—real fucking hard—again, pun intended.

Thank fuck there are no cops out tonight because I would have been locked up for reckless driving. I've never driven so fast in my life. No sooner do I pull into my spot back at school than I lean over the center console and shove my face between Quinn's thighs. As soon as my tongue hits her clit, she grinds her pussy against my face and comes, screaming my name when she does.

Sitting up, I wipe my mouth with the back of my hand and stare over at a sated Quinn. "You ready for more, babe?"

She nods and smiles. "Do you want me to attend to that," she points to my dick, "before we head inside?"

"As much as I'd love a blow job from you, I want to feel your pussy slide down my dick and then I want to fuck you into the middle of next week."

"Then let's go."

She picks up her panties from the floorboard and climbs out, flashing me her ass before she pulls her skirt down.

Meeting her by the hood of my car, I lace our fingers together and we head up to my room. Before the door has clicked closed, Quinn is standing before me naked. My eyes focus on her uniform skirt that is pooled at her feet. Sliding my gaze up her legs, I stare at her shaved cunt. Her slit is still glistening, and I lick my lips. Raking my eyes up farther, I pass over her bump and up to her tits. Her glorious tits. Stepping to her, I lift my hand and cup her mound in my palm. She moans when I give it a gentle squeeze. Lowering my head, I take her nipple into my mouth and suck. Kissing over to her other breast, I do the same again. For a few minutes, I focus on her tits. Alternating between the two. "Please," she moans, pressing her thighs together.

"Please what?" I ask, standing to full height, staring into her eyes.

"I need you," she pants.

"You have me," I tell her, and I mean it. We may fight like cats and dogs at times because she's a psycho bitch and I'm an asshole, but I wouldn't change a thing. Quinn is mine, there's no changing that fact.

"You have too many clothes on," she informs me, gripping the hem of my shirt and lifting it up. Her nails rake over my abs. Grabbing the material by the scruff of the collar at my neck, I pull my shirt off and drop it to the floor.

"That move is so hot," Quinn says, ogling my chest.

"What move?"

"When guys take their shirt off like that. So. Fucking. Hot."

"Duly noted and I will be sure to remove my shirts that way for the rest of time. Is there a sexy way to remove pants?"

She shakes her head and bites her lip, watching as I flip open the button and lower my fly. Gripping the waistband of my pants and briefs, I remove both in one fell swoop and step out of them, leaving me as naked as Quinn.

We move toward one another and our lips slam together. Our tongues slip and slide in and out of each other's mouths. Hands roam each other's bodies. My cock hardens between us. Quinn reaches down and grips my shaft, squeezing the tip in her palm, causing me to hiss into her mouth.

Walking her backward toward my bed, I spin when we reach it and sit down, bringing Quinn with me. She straddles me and not once do our lips part. She lifts herself up and rubs the head of my dick with her pussy. There is no better feel than a cunt hugging your dick, and Quinn's cunt was made for my dick. She pulls back and stares into my eyes. Resting her hands on my shoulders, with her eyes locked on mine, she slides down until she's fully seated. She begins to ride me, bucking up and down, grinding her clit against my pubic bone on each downward ministration. She throws her head back in ecstasy and she's never looked more fucking radiant. "I love you," I murmur as I lean forward and lick up her neck.

"Love you too," she breathlessly pants. "So fucking much."

Pressing my lips to hers again, I kiss her as she continues to ride me. Her walls clench around me, and I know she's close. Her breathing escalates, her cheeks are flushed, and her skin glistens with sweat.

"I'm coming," she moans, wrapping her arms around my neck, pulling me into her. Her tits mash against my chest, and her cunt squeezes my dick setting off my release too. Together we tumble over the edge, moaning and groaning as we ride the pleasure wave.

Collapsing back to the mattress, Quinn comes with me and lies on my chest. She places a kiss on my chest, lifts her head, and stares down at me. "That was amazing," she says, her face content.

"It's always amazing, baby, 'cause you and I are amazing together."

"We are, aren't we?" I nod in agreement. "Why didn't we give this a real go sooner?"

"'Cause I'm a dickhead."

"And I'm a bitch."

"But you're my bitch and I'm never letting you go."

"And you're my dickhead, and Tootsie and I are so lucky to have you."

She lowers her head back to my chest, and a few moments later, she's sound asleep.

As much as I love having her naked body plastered to me, I need to take a piss. Sliding her off me, she snuggles into the blanket when I cover her up. She looks so peaceful, and I can't help but smile.

Heading into my adjoining bathroom, I take a piss,

climb back into bed, and snuggle with my baby momma. Life is great right now and nothing will bring me down.

QUINN

"I WANTED TOOTSIE ROLLS, NOT POPS," I scream at Hendrix like a banshee, throwing the package of pops at his stupid sexy face.

"What's the difference?" he asks, and his question irritates me further.

"One is on a stick with a crunchy outer and chewy center. The other is a chewy morsel of goodness with no stick."

"They both have chewiness, just suck the pop and get to the chewy bit."

"You fucking suck it. Why didn't you just get me rolls?"

"The mini mart was out."

"So go somewhere else," I snap at him. "They have other stores in Crestwood." I know I'm being irrational right now, but I want a Tootsie Roll, not a fucking Tootsie Pop.

"Well, fucking get them yourself then, you ungrateful bitch," he sneers back at me.

"Did you just call me a bitch?"

"If the bitch shoe fits, I will call you a bitch."

"You're a cunt, Hendrix Vanderbelt. A fucking cunt. Get the fuck out of my sight before I kick you in the nuts."

"With fucking pleasure." He storms out of my room, slamming my door behind him.

Standing here, I stare at the closed door and my eyes well with tears. Letting out a wail, I collapse to the floor and begin to cry. This is the one part of pregnancy I hate, the hormones. One minute I'm up, and the next, I'm losing my shit over a Tootsie Pop. A fucking Tootsie Pop.

Sitting up, I lean against my bed, resting my hand on my bump. "Did I just ruin us?" I ask my belly. Tootsie gives me a kick. "Is that you agreeing or disagreeing?" I'm rewarded with another kick. There is no better feeling than when Tootsie kicks. The first time she did, I had no clue what it was, but it scared the absolute shit out of me, and now, I can't wait to feel them. I also love when Tootsie gets the hiccups, it feels like a million butterflies taking flight in my stomach.

Dropping my head back, I rub my belly and think about Hendrix and the fact I may have just ruined us over a Tootsie Pop.

Reaching over, I grab the package, unwrap one, and

pop it into my mouth. See, I'm a fucking psycho. Hendrix is going to leave me, and I'll be raising this baby alone.

Climbing up onto my bed, I hug my knees to my chest, suck on my Tootsie Pop—which is yummy by the way—and wonder what I can do to make this up to Hendrix.

As I sit here sucking on my Tootsie Pop, an idea forms. I know exactly what I'm going to do to make it up to Hendrix for being a raging hormonal bitch just now. Reaching over, I grab my phone and bring up Google.

Ten minutes later, my gift has been designed and once I'm happy, I hit order. I really hope Hendrix loves it.

HENDRIX

"FUCK, FUCK, FUCKITY FUCK," I snap. Saint
frowns, staring after me as I slam my locker shut.

"You okay?" he finally asks after he realizes I won't
bite his head off.

"I just keep fucking things up with Quinn. She gets
upset over the smallest things, and I feel like no matter
what I do I piss her off."

Saint scoffs, shaking his head. "Yeah, well, that's just
women in particular, add in hormones and all that crazy
pregnancy stuff, I'm surprised you and Quinn haven't torn

each other apart. I mean, you guys are best known for your public outbursts." He raises his fingers and air quotes outbursts. Shoving him against the lockers, he laughs then throws his arm around my neck pulling me into him, trying to wrestle me. We stumble and fall to the floor in a heap. I grunt when Saint lands on me, muscly fucker is heavy.

"Jesus, how much do you fucking weigh?" I groan, holding my side. Shoving me, Saint slaps me around the head and leans down harder on me.

"Why are you on the floor?" Thatcher asks, looking down at us.

"This fucker wanted to wrestle and you know I can't refuse a fight, so I took this fucker to the ground." I slap Saint's side, making him groan.

"Umm, I took you down. You're getting soft in your old age," he teases before pushing himself up and off of me. I stay down on the floor, too exhausted to move right now.

"I'm surprised you even came up for air, you know with how your tongue is permanently down Remy's throat and all." Saint chuckles, causing Thatcher to shove him hard, forcing him to stumble.

"Hey, fucker," Saint barks. Rubbing his arm, he pushes Thatch aside, steps over me, and heads to class. Looking back at Thatch, I see him run his gaze over me. "You good?" he questions.

"Yes, no, not really."

"Quinn?" he asks, and I nod. He looks at me in a 'well, what did you do' kind of way.

"I keep messing shit up with her."

"Well, messing shit up with women is our specialty."

Thatcher chuckles. He offers me his hand and pulls me up. I wait for any wisdom from my brother but the fucker stays quiet.

Grabbing my books from my locker, the two of us walk together to class. I'm lost in my head, thinking about Quinn and yesterday, and I become pissed that she got upset over something as simple as Tootsie Rolls. She may be a wee thing compared to me, but that girl definitely scares me, not that I'd admit that to anyone, especially my brothers.

When Thatcher and I walk into Calculus, I notice we have a substitute. She nods hello and I continue on to my desk.

Rian's head is down and I can't resist the temptation to flick his ear as I shuffle by. He curses, holding his hand over it to protect himself and I begin to chuckle when he grumbles, "Fucker."

He seems better today, but knowing my cousin is still hurting fucking kills me. Rian has always been like a brother to us, and when one of us hurts we all hurt. Leaning into him whispering so we don't have unwanted attention, I ask, "Are you seeing that therapist?"

He lifts his head, nods and sighs dramatically. "I'm fine, Hendrix." I scoff loudly, catching the attention of the class. All eyes are now on us, including the professor's.

"Sorry," I offer as an apology. It appeases the teacher, and he goes back to the lesson but I can do this shit in my sleep. I much prefer Mrs. Mosttert's way of teaching, but she's away and we are stuck with this substitute.

"Fine, my ass," I say, leaning into Rian when everyone is once again focused on the assignment on the board. "You were so off your head the other day you could barely function, and now suddenly, you're fine. I call bullshit."

Ri ignores me, and it's probably for the best he does. Things usually get heated pretty quickly between us Vanderbelts.

Thatcher taps my shoulder from behind me. Pointing his pen at Ri, he gestures and then mouths, "He okay?"

Shrugging, I look to Ri and then back at Thatcher, causing Ri to sigh. "I know you fuckers are talking about me, but really, I'm fine."

"We're just concerned, man," I tell him honestly.

"I'm fine," he says again, this time with force.

"Boys, if this chitchat continues, I will have to ask you to leave," the teacher says, causing the three of us to roll our eyes. This bitch clearly doesn't know who we are, but I'm not in the mood for detention, so I rein in my anger and salute her, smiling sweetly. She blushes and I turn my focus back to the board. I stare at the board, but nothing registers in my brain, and to be honest, right now, I don't give a flying fuck about the square root of pie or whatever this task is about. All I care about is Quinn and Tootsie.

By the time class ends, I'm ready to get out of here and rush out. I need to get back to Quinn and fix Tootsie Pop Gate.

"Hendrix, wait up," Remy shouts behind me when I enter the corridor, and from the tone of her voice, it seems important. She's been through a lot lately with her brother returning from the grave, but that wasn't the craziest thing relating to Arlen Hearst. Turns out, he was in love with our dad. When Dad rejected him, he killed Dad in a fit of rage, I presume, and then tried to kill Reign's partners when he decided he wanted Reign again—ohh yeah, Reign is bi and currently is in a threesome relationship with Alani Thomas and Hudson Finley. After Alani and Hudson were rescued from being held captive by Arlen, they locked him away at Crestwood Asylum where he was recently diagnosed as a schizophrenic. That's a lot for one person to handle, but Remy is a tough, cool chick. Hell, she has Thatcher wrapped around her little finge,r so bonus points there. I spin on my heel and wait for her to catch up.

"What's up, Rem?" I ask when she reaches me, but I start walking again and continue on my way to Quinn's room.

"I heard you're worried about you and Quinn." I stop and glare down at her. She heard? More like Thatcher gave her the details, fucker. She holds up her hands in surrender but continues, "Look, I just wanted to give you some advice from a girl's perspective."

"Okay, fine," I agree and realize this could be good for me.

"Don't put so much pressure on yourself, Hendrix, and give Quinn a break." I go to interrupt, but she raises her hand, and gives me a look that says 'shut your piehole and listen,' so I do as I'm told and zip it. "Look, Quinn has a lot of hormones flowing through her right now. Things are confusing and complicated—"

"And by complicated," I interrupt, "you mean that the baby isn't mine?"

"What?" she screeches, her eyes widen with shock. Seems Quinn didn't tell her and now me and my big mouth have spilled the beans. Shit, another thing for Quinn to be mad at me over. "No, that's not what I meant, but holy fuck, that's crazy, and it's so good of you to step up."

"I'd do anything for her, Rem."

She smiles. "She's lucky to have you, and we will loop back to that bomb in a hot minute, but being a senior in high school is tough enough as it is. Add in a pregnancy, and it seems no baby daddy—"

"I'm the baby daddy," I growl, and I think I've shocked her.

"Look, Hendrix, sometimes bio parents aren't the best, you as well as anyone knows that. All that matters is that you'll be there for that kid and her, but what I meant by complicated, she's been put on bed rest after a really scary moment. Then add in all the stuff that happened with her parents and you getting pops and not rolls, it's confusing for her. One minute she hates you and then the next she loves and wants to fuck you. It's a lot to process."

"Yeah, I know," I say, running my fingers through my hair, "but how do I fix it? What do I do to ease all this for her?"

Then Remy shocks the shit out of me with what her solution is. "We need to throw her a baby shower." It was a statement, not a suggestion, and as I think over her idea, the more I like it.

A smile forms on my face, but then it falls because I have no fucking clue how to host a baby shower. Like, wouldn't you do it after the baby arrives since there's nothing to shower?

"Sounds good, Rem, but, ummm, you'll help me? Right? Because I don't know the first thing about baby showers."

"Of course, I will," Remy states matter-of-factly.

"Thank fuck 'cause how do you do that with no baby to shower?"

Remy bursts out laughing. "You don't actually shower a baby. You shower the baby and the baby momma in gifts."

"Ohhh, right, that makes more sense."

Linking arms with me, she guides me toward the cafeteria and 'Operation Baby Shower' commences.

QUINN

IT'S BEEN a few days since Tootsie Pop Gate and Hendrix has been MIA, aka avoiding me. I'm starting to panic my Tootsie Pop meltdown was the straw that broke the camel's back, and I've really fucked this up with him. He's been nothing but amazing since I told him I was pregnant, and a fucking Tootsie Pop is going to be the thing that tears us apart.

The tears stream down my cheeks and I fall to the carpet of my room. Leaning against my bed, I pop a Tootsie Pop into my mouth and wallow in self-pity for being such a whorebag bitch.

Deciding I need to get myself out of this funk, I dry my tears, but then an ad for a local rescue center comes through Spotify and I start to cry again. I can't help the crazy emotions coming from me right now.

A soft knock pulls me from my inner thoughts about Hendrix and me and rescue dogs, and I climb to my feet.

Opening the door, Remy's face falls when she sees mine. "Quinn, oh my God what's wrong?" I sniff while she lets herself in, coming straight for me and wrapping me in her arms.

"Hendrix hates me," I sob.

"Oh, no, no he doesn't," she says, trying her best to comfort me. Remy smiles and grabs my hands in hers, she squeezes in that reassuring kind of way, but at the moment, it does little to reassure me. "Babe, I promise you he doesn't hate you. Why don't you fix your face and come with me? I have a surprise for you."

"You do?" I murmur, excitement building at the prospect of a surprise for me. See, I'm psycho, one minute I'm down and the next I'm excited. She nods and ushers me to my makeup chair.

Looking at my reflection, my eyes widen when I take in my appearance. I look like a sea hag who's just been through a hurricane and a tsunami. Doing as she asks, I fix my face and wonder what my surprise could be. God only knows what this girl has planned, but for the first time in days, I'm excited.

That excitement from earlier turns into complete and utter shock when I see the entire room is decked out in baby decorations and there are balloons spelling out 'Tootsie' and 'Quinn' and 'Hendrix.' Tears fill my eyes, and the moment I see Hendrix walk toward me with a bouquet of flowers in his arms, my tears turn into full-blown sobs.

Hendrix pulls me into his arms and hugs me. He pulls back, slides his hand through my hair, and brings my head toward him. He covers my mouth with his and kisses me until I'm completely breathless.

The moment he pulls back and breaks the kiss, I mutter, "I … I thought you hated me?" My eyes well with tears again and when I see Hendrix frown, a tear falls down my cheek. Lifting his hand, he wipes away the lone droplet and kisses me again, showing me with his mouth that he does not hate me.

"This is what we do, baby. We love and we hate. We fight and then we fuck, but, Quinn, My Queen, you're mine and I am yours and only yours."

His lips take mine again, and then Remy breaks it by smacking Hendrix on the arm.

"Stop sucking her face, we planned an amazing baby shower, and she needs to see more than just your face."

Hendrix chuckles and takes my hand, pulling me toward the table that's covered with food, including Tootsie Rolls with a little sign that states, "Quinn's Tootsie Rolls, Do Not Touch." I chuckle, pick one up, unwrap it, and pop it into my mouth. Grabbing his hand again, I hold it between mine and look up at him. Nothing but love surrounds us. Pushing up to my tippy-toes, I place a kiss on his jaw.

"Thank you," I tell him, my heart feeling full right now.

"You should thank them." He nods to Remy, Alani, Rowan, and Hudson. "They did most of it, I mean, I helped, but the girls and Hudson did all the decorating." He seems so proud right now, he's almost glowing. "I did the food," he adds, smiling down at me.

"You did the food?" I ask, surprised he even wanted to throw me a baby shower. He nods, and in that moment, I couldn't love him more than I do right now. He really is the best, stepping up when I was all alone. I hate we are lying to everyone. Well, everyone but Remy since Hendrix blurted it out the other day, but at the same time, I'm not because I could not do this without him. He is literally my knight in shining armor, swooping in and saving Tootsie and me.

We spend the afternoon mingling with our friends, celebrating the upcoming arrival of Tootsie. I'm down to opening the last of the presents when Remy gets up and smiles. "Okay, there is one more small surprise." Thatcher chuckles, and I have a feeling Rem's version of small is anything but. Thatcher and Hendrix head out of the room, and then I almost fall off my chair when Remy's *small* surprise comes through the door.

"Is that a … a giraffe?" I giggle.

"Yep," Remy confirms matter-of-factly, smiling like a carnival clown.

"Oh, my God." I laugh out loud, covering my mouth, trying my best not to give Remy the wrong impression because I love it so, so much.

"This is freakin' amazing," I tell her. "Thank you so much … for the giraffe and my shower." I smile brightly at her, and she gives me a smile of her own, but at the same time, she shrugs like it's no big deal.

"That thing is massive." Hudson chuckles.

"That's what you said last night," Reign whispers to Huddy Boy, but it's not so much of a whisper and the entire room erupts into laughter.

"Calm down, big boy." Alani pats Reign's knee, earning herself a smack on her ass when she bends down to grab the gift she has for us. Glaring back at him, she gives him a look of warning, and from the look on Reign's face, he knows he's in trouble but then he throws her a wink and all anger evaporates from her.

She hands me the gift, and I open their present. "Oh, wow, thank you," I tell them, pulling out a one-of-a-kind onesie with 'Baby Vanderbelt' printed across the front.

Staring at the pile of presents, I shake my head. My friends have gone completely mad. This baby has so much and he, or she, isn't even here yet. Today, Tootsie, Hendrix, and I have been spoiled rotten, and I have a feeling it will continue since we are the first pregnancy in the group. He or she is going to be one spoiled and doted on little Vanderbelt.

An idea forms and before I can think on it, I say to the room, "I have to go grab something real quick." Before anyone can say anything, I race out of the room as if my ass was on fire. Hendrix's brow dips but now is the perfect time to give him the gift I ordered for him.

Racing to my room, well as quickly as a pregnant lady can race, I grab the gift and head back down to where Hendrix and everyone is waiting. When I walk back into the room, Hendrix's eyebrows raise when I stop in front of him with the gift box in my hands, pushing my hands out, I hand the box to him.

"What's this?" he asks.

"Open it and you'll find out," I say.

His gaze scans over the rectangular black box with a

massive orange bow on top. Placing it on the table next to him, he begins to unwrap it and we all intently watch as he finally pulls the last piece of wrapping paper off. Confused and slightly amused, he lifts the lid on the box and slowly pulls out the frame.

"Quinn," he whispers my name and smiles brightly. He holds up the frame and scans the print. I got him a customized architectural name print. This customized print pays full appreciation to ornamental volutes, lintels and arches, using their unique shapes to spell out his name, or so the website I ordered it from said.

Hendrix chuckles and smiles brightly, "I fucking love it, Quinn. Absolutely love it."

"You do?" I ask, hesitation lacing my voice. He nods, staring down at the print again.

"Very much so. It's perfect." He looks up at me and the smile on his face is wide and I can tell he means it. He pulls me into his side and hugs me with one arm, kissing me on the head.

Placing the gift back into the box, I look around at our friends here today. Before I get a chance to thank everyone for being here and the gifts, Hendrix shares some more exciting news. "This gift, this perfect gift goes with the news I got earlier today."

"What news?" I ask.

"I, umm, I've been accepted early to Crestwood University of Technology to study architectural design next year."

My eyes widen at his news and I jump at Hendrix hugging him.

"That's amazing, baby." I tell him, "I'm so happy for you." He places his fingers under my chin and kisses me.

Once we pull apart, together with our friends we

continue to celebrate the upcoming arrival of Tootsie and Hendrix's achievement. He truly is incredible and I could not be more proud of him.

"Today was amazing," I say, laying my head on Hendrix's shoulder later that evening in his room. "We celebrated Tootsie. You got your gift AAAAAND an early acceptance into university. Life is great right now." And as soon as those words pass my lips, I hope I didn't jinx anything. Life has a way of fucking you up the ass sideways when things are going well and you voice it aloud. I really hope I didn't ruin our lucky streak with my slip of the tongue.

"I'm glad you enjoyed it, babe."

"I did. Thank you again. It was such a surprise." And to show my appreciation, I lean over and place a kiss on his lips. "Now, why don't we finish the day by making me feel even better," I mutter as I reach up and guide his head toward my pussy.

"With pleasure," he growls and in the blink of an eye, I'm on my back and Hendrix is between my thighs. He pulls my underwear down and groans when he sees my arousal glistening in the dim light of his room.

He shuffles between my legs, leans down, and his tongue flicks over my clit, causing me to hiss at the sensation of his tongue sliding over my bundle of nerves. I can't help it and my thighs push together, trapping his head. He licks me again and again and within minutes, my body is convulsing. My legs are shaking as his tongue, his delectable tongue, drives me wild. He drives me to the edge, and I reach that point where I can't hold back anymore, and I shatter. Squeezing his head tighter with my thighs, I scream his name as I explode.

Today was amazing in every way, and it's all due to the man between my thighs. Tootsie and I are so lucky to have him and our amazing friends.

HENDRIX

MOM HAS SUMMONED us to dinner, and unlike when Dad would summon us, I'm excited to head to our childhood home.

Quinn is in the passenger seat next to me. She's wearing an orange spaghetti strap sundress that showcases her tits perfectly, and I want nothing more than to bury my face into them.

"You all right there, staring at my chest?"

"Perfectly happy, thank you very much. You think we have time to pull over and I can bury my face in them?"

"As much as it pains me to say so, you will have to wait. I need to pee and eat."

"Fine," I huff. "Lucky I love you and your tits."

"And we love you, too, but I really need to pee, and if you don't want me to ruin the upholstery, step on the gas."

Not wanting piss in my car, I plant my foot down, and we make it to Mom's in record time.

Before the car has come to a halt, Quinn is out and racing up the front steps. She knocks, and as soon as Lisette opens the door, Quinn pushes past her and races inside.

"Bathroom," I say as I wander up the stairs, smiling at Lisette.

She giggles and lets me in. "Everyone is out by the pool."

Nodding, I walk inside just as Quinn comes out. "Better?"

"Much, but I'm still starving," she says.

"I'll bring snacks out soon. Dinner is still a ways off," Lisette says as she heads toward the kitchen.

"You're the best, Lisette," Quinn calls out.

Taking her hand in mine, we head outside and meet up with Mom, Thatcher, Rem, Reign, Alani, Hudson, and Saint. The girls are on loungers with Mom, and my brothers and Hudson are in the pool splashing about. Kissing Mom on the cheek, I pull my shirt over my head in the way Quinn has told me is 'sexy as hell.' Looking at her, I throw her a wink and then cannonball into the pool, splashing the girls and Mom. They all squeal and all us boys laugh, but my laughter dies when I look over and see Quinn standing there in a barely-there, bright orange bikini. Her teeny tiny bump looks amazing, as do her tits. She turns around and I stifle a groan when I see her ass.

The bottoms of her bikini are barely there, they are more than a G-string but still show a lot of ass.

"Looking good, Quinn," Saint calls out.

Swimming over, I punch him in the arm. "Mine," I growl.

"I can appreciate a fine ass, and Quinn has a mighty fine booty." He says that last part loud enough for her to hear.

"Thanks, Saintly," Quinn shouts back, "but I'm taken." She looks at me and winks before she lies back on a lounger. Lisette brings out the food and heads back inside. A few moments later, she returns with another plate and takes it to Quinn. Quinn's eyes widen and her face lights up. She sits up, crosses her legs, and pulls the plate closer to her. She picks up a carrot stick and nibbles on it.

Standing in the pool, I watch her eat her plate.

"You're so whipped," Thatcher says, splashing me.

"Says the whipped one," I throw at him before splashing him back.

"Too fucking right I am," Thatcher proudly says before he shouts, "I love Remington Hearst," causing all the girls to look at us with confusion on their faces.

"You've gone soft, man," Reign teases. "You were the king of fuck and chuck."

"I was, this is true, but I was just searching for the one and when Remy came into my life, I passed that title on to, well, none of you fuckers 'cause you're all whipped too." Processing his words, I smile because I feel that statement deep in my bones … just without the manwhore status. From the first moment I laid eyes on Quinn Ellis, I was smitten. Yes, our path to our happily ever after has been bumpy, and yes, it's currently sporting a lie, but at the end of the day, we love one another and that's all that matters.

"How's your sister doing, Hudson?" Mom asks as we're all seated around the dinner table. Our plates are empty, and our tummies are full. Lisette is a fantastic cook, and I wonder if I can poach her from Mom to cook for Quinn, me, and the baby. I chuckle to myself because that will never happen. Lisette has been with Mom since Mom was a little girl, and she will work for Mom until the day she dies.

I tune back into Hudson telling Mom about his, Reign, and Alani's trip to New York for her showcase later this month.

"We should all go," I blurt out.

"You wanna go to New York? For a dance thing?" Reign asks, his tone laced with shock that I suggested it.

"Well, yeah. It can be one last hurrah for Quinn before Tootsie arrives."

"That would be great," Quinn says. "But can I fly while pregnant?"

"According to the baby book, you are fine to fly up till the third trimester."

"Look at you, being all daddy-like," Reign teases me, but I brush him off.

"When Alani gets pregnant, you will read all the books so you know what to expect." I pause. "Did you know when a woman is pregnant, her heart grows bigger physically as well as metaphorically?"

"I call bullshit," Thatcher voices.

"It's true," Mom backs me up. "Because your blood

level increases by forty to fifty percent, your heart needs the extra help, otherwise, it'd be working harder and faster, and growing a baby is hard enough as it is."

"So, what does everyone think?" I ask when the conversation turns away from women's bodies and growing babies. "Are we doing this New York thing?"

Everyone agrees, and Hudson takes on the task of booking everything since he has all the details about the showcase.

The rest of the evening is filled with random useless facts, and I think the most intriguing one is turtles breathe through their butts. I cannot wait to drop that into a conversation one of these days.

Quinn and I say goodnight to everyone when she yawns for the millionth time. She falls asleep on the trip back to school, and when I pull into my spot, I just sit here, staring at a peaceful sleeping Quinn. A warmth spreads through my body and I find myself relaxed and happy, I hope this feeling never goes away.

QUINN

HENDRIX SMILES over at me as we touch down in New York, we've come to see Lauren's show and I'm excited to be back. I love New York, and this will probably be my last trip away before the baby comes.

Rowan and Saint have been arguing since we boarded. I'm kind of glad it's them and not Hendrix and me because normally we're at each other's throats, but since my surprise baby shower the other week, things between us have been great.

Saint growls, "For fuck's sake, Ro, just listen." Rowan

tries her best to hold back the tears, but she can't hide her face fast enough before one slides down her cheek.

"Come on, baby, please don't cry," Saints apologizes and takes her hand, gripping it tightly in his. I watch the anguish mar his face as he comforts her. Whatever is going on between them is serious, and I hate I haven't been there for my friend in her time of need, and as if he's in my head, Hendrix leans into me.

"They'll work it out, they always do," Hendrix whispers so only I can hear. He's right. I know that because Saint and Rowan are like us—they're bad for each other, but at the same time, they're perfect for each other. And like us, they just need to pull their heads out of their asses and get their shit together.

"Hello, New York!" Rian shouts as he exits the plane and skips down the airstairs. Then he walks, no stalks, across the tarmac like a freakin' rockstar and climbs into the waiting car. He invited himself along when he found out we were coming and no one wanted to tell him no. He's had it rough these last few months, his whole world has been rocked and I really feel for the guy.

We all follow Rian and pile in after him. Rowan chooses to sit next to me instead of Saint. Clearly whatever they were arguing about isn't over. Placing my hand in hers, I give it a reassuring squeeze.

She smiles over at me, resting her head on my shoulder. She's exhausted and the terrible feeling of being an awful friend sits heavily on my chest. I should have been there for my friend, and I decide on this trip, I will be.

We're waiting in the hotel lobby while Thatcher checks us all in, getting the room keys. He returns and hands them out to the guys. Hendrix grabs his and turns to face me, winks my way, and holds up our room key. He gives me a smoldering look that has my panties dampening and my clit throbbing. "You ready, baby?" he says, taking me in his arms and kissing me like it'll be the last time.

"So fucking ready." But then I hear Saint and I'm torn over what to do.

"Please just come, Ro." Saint sighs. His hand runs across his face, and I know it's going to take some extra special groveling to fix this. Rowan storms off toward the elevators with Saint racing behind her, maybe some hot make-up sex is what they need. So I decide to stay where I am with Hendrix … and hopefully get some hot sex of my own.

Hendrix pulls me to his side, and we walk over to the elevators. He pushes the call button and the doors immediately open. He drags me inside and presses the button for our floor. Then he pulls me into his arms, my back to his front. He kisses behind my ear and growls, "As soon as we get into our room, I'm going to eat that pussy of yours until everyone on our floor can hear you scream my name."

"Yes, please,' I breathlessly pant. If I thought I was buzzing and wet before, now I'm vibrating and soaked. The moment the doors ping open, I drag him out into the corridor. Dropping my bag, I push him against the wall, grip his cheeks in my palms, and kiss him passionately. Breaking the kiss, I lift onto my toes and whisper, "You better not come up for air until I've had at least six orgasms, Hendrix Vanderbelt."

"Yes, ma'am," he mutters and cements our deal with another kiss. He kisses me until we're both breathless and we are dry humping one another. Bending down, he picks up my bag, takes my hand, and leads us to our room.

Once inside, he unceremoniously drops our bags in the

doorway and proceeds to strip me naked. His lips trail down my body, kissing every inch of my skin he can until his lips ghost my pussy. I moan when he brushes against me, but he doesn't go any farther. Gripping his hair, I'm ready to pull strands out when his tongue darts out and slides over me, causing me to moan like a wanton hussy. Taking my clit between his lips, he sucks and gently nips my sensitive bundle of nerves. I cry out when he pushes his tongue inside me, the friction sets me off and my body shakes with pleasure. I feel Hendrix grin against me and knowing he's accepted my challenge, I smile. He won't stop until I'm completely satisfied and I'm a-o-fucking-k with that.

A few hours later, I'm a blithering mess because Hendrix has just drawn orgasm number five from me without using his dick. He pushes two fingers inside me, and when he sucks my clit, orgasm six begins to build. He continues to finger fuck and suck me and just when I'm about to explode, he stops. My eyes widen in displeasure, and I'm about to let him have it when he plunges his cock inside me.

"Fuck," we both groan at the sensation of his dick sliding into me.

Thrusting his hips forward, he repeats the motion over and over, bringing me closer and closer to the edge. He bends down, taking my lips with his. His tongue tangles with mine and we groan and pant as we both reach the point of no return, and together we come.

Hendrix moves off me, lying by my side, and panting heavily. I slide toward him, resting my head on his shoulder. "That was …" I breathe.

"Mind-blowing," Hendrix says, finishing my sentence for me.

We lie there for a few moments, catching our breaths, until I glance at the time and realize we're going to be late if we don't climb out of bed. "We need to get up and get ready, otherwise we'll be late."

"Mmmhmpf," he mumbles, making no effort to move. Slapping his leg, Hendrix just groans. Shaking my head, I climb out of bed, and he manages to slap my ass before I head to the bathroom for a shower.

"I'm not done filling you, Quinn Ellis," he says, watching me from the bed.

"For now you are. My va-jay-jay needs a break, but you can totally fill me back up again after the show."

"Deal," he replies with a chuckle.

Climbing off the bed, he walks into the bathroom and moves behind me, kissing my neck and cupping my boobs. When his dick hardens and presses into my ass, everything else fades away … looks like we are going to be late after all.

Watching Lauren on stage was incredible. The way she moves is magical. I was hypnotized by the way her body bent and moved in time with the music.

The show has just finished, and everyone is on their feet clapping.

"Whooooo!" Hudson shouts, cupping his hands together making the sound travel all the way to the stage, causing his sister to blush.

Alani kisses his cheek and then raises her hands in the air, applauding Lauren and the rest of the dancers.

"Damn." Remy smiles. "That was amazing."

"Right?" I reply.

We all make our way out of the theater and wait for Lauren and her castmates to join us so we can head out and celebrate.

"Hey, guys," she says with a wide smile as she exits the theater.

Hudson lifts Lauren in his arms, spinning her around.

"Fuck, Lo, you were incredible." She giggles, hugging her brother before moving around everyone and doing the same.

"You were amazing," I say, kissing her cheek.

"Thanks, Quinn." Her smile is just as wide when she reaches me. She wraps her arms around me and then drops her hands to my belly. "Look at your bump, it's so cute."

Lauren moves back to her brother, and he throws his arm around her shoulder, pulling her into him. He kisses the top of her head before reaching for Reign's hand while Alani comes to Reign's other side and takes his other hand. Watching the way they navigate collectively is fascinating. Seeing the three of them together is still weird, but they do make a beautiful throuple.

"Time to party," Thatcher shouts once Lauren is all hugged out.

Remy shakes her head at her boyfriend, but from the smile she's throwing at him, she's down to party too. Knowing tonight I'll be the only one not drinking is a strange feeling, but weirdly I'm okay with it.

It's after eleven by the time we enter the club. Hendrix is close by, letting me have space but not letting me get too far ahead. That is until Remy drags Alani and me to the dance floor. I grab Rowan's hand and Alani grabs

Lauren's, and we all dance together while the boys find a booth and sit down to watch us.

After a few songs, I'm enjoying myself and not even slightly annoyed the other girls have had three drinks each already and I'm drinking lime and soda ... sans vodka.

Looking up, my gaze connects with Hendrix's. He winks at me, and in return, I blow him a kiss. Lifting my hands and running them through my hair, I dance for him. Everything around me fades away and it's just the two of us.

Lauren grabs my hand, and I turn away from Hendrix and begin to dance with her. Bumping and grinding against her, I'm having a blast when hands slide around my waist, resting on my hips. I was wondering when he was going to come and join me so maybe we can recreate what happened at a party a couple of years ago. Looking down at the hands on me, I furrow my brow because they look different. When I lift my gaze, I see Lauren and notice her eyes are wide open, and her mouth is in a shocked 'ohh.'

Cautiously, I spin around and now it's my turn for my eyes and mouth to drop open in shock as I stare at the man before me. Standing before me is him, look-alike Hendrix.

Ohh fuck!

HENDRIX

WATCHING Quinn dance with her friends is a sight to be seen. Her hips move and sway to the beat and she looks fucking hot. She's wearing a figure-hugging baby blue dress that leaves very little to the imagination, and when she spins around, I get a glimpse of her bump and my grin widens. Pregnancy agrees with her, and I wish with everything in me the baby was mine, but it seems fate has other ideas.

And with the Rian and Risa scenario, I will not let a day go by that I don't tell this kid I love him or her, and as soon as they are old enough to understand, I will tell them the truth. The image of Rian's face when his parentage came to light is one that will be seared into my brain forever. He was hurt and I don't want that for our child.

Quinn spins around, and we make eye contact through the busy club. Her eyes lock on to me, and she begins to sway her hips as she dances just for me. She bites her lip and I'm sure she's thinking about that one time at a party …

… *Quinn and Rowan are dancing up a storm. Every guy in this place is watching the two of them dance seductively together. A guy moves in and puts his hands on Quinn's hips, grinding his cock into her ass.*

I see red.

Marching over, I grip his arm and pull him away from her before I throw him across the dance floor. I'm about to go over to him and pummel him for touching what's mine when a slightly tipsy Quinn giggles.

My gaze flicks from the touchy asshole to Quinn. "You think that's funny, Quinn?"

She shrugs at me, and we silently stare at one another while everyone continues to dance around us. She lifts her hand and beckons me to her with her index finger, and like a moth to a flame, I go to her.

Stopping in front of her, I place my hands on her hips and pull her into me. My body moves in time with hers. Pulling her closer to me, I slide my leg between her thighs. She drapes her arms over my shoulders and begins to grind herself on me.

Leaning down, I nibble along her jawline to her ear and whisper, "I'm going to finger fuck you here in the middle of the dance floor. If you can come quietly, I'll then take you upstairs and fuck you where I want you to scream my name for everyone to hear. Every person at this party will know what we are doing, and they'll all be jealous of you."

She stares at me, her eyes full of hunger. She licks her lips and waggles her eyebrows at me. "Have at it, big boy."

And have at it I do.

Pulling her into my chest, I slam my lips to her and run my hand down her side to the hem of her barely-there, figure-hugging dress. Sliding my hand under the material of her dress, I trace my fingertips up her thigh. Her skin prickles with goose-bumps. My eyes widen when I find her pussy is bare.

"Where are your panties, Quinn?"

"I'm not wearing any, VPL."

"V P what?"

"Visible panty line," she says, as if I know what the hell that means. "I didn't want anything to distract from the dress, hence no panties ... or bra."

"I should spank you for that, but you'd like that too much."

"I so wou—" She doesn't finish her sentence because I thrust a finger deep inside her. Pumping my digit in and out a few times, I add a second finger when she demands more. She lowers her head to where my shoulder meets my neck and bites down, holding back her scream as she comes all over my fingers.

She lifts her head and stares at me, completely blissed out from coming. "I won, so I'm gonna need you to fuck me now."

"A deal's a deal," I tell her as I pull my hand out from her cunt and lift it to my mouth to suck her release off my fingers, but she grabs my wrist and guides my hand to her mouth. She sucks my fingers clean and then kisses me. I can taste her on her lips and the need to fuck her slams into me like a freight train.

Lifting her up, she wraps her legs around me, and I make my way to the stairs. Everyone hoots and hollers as I take her upstairs for part two of the evening ...

• • •

With that memory fresh in my mind, I stand up to recreate that moment, but I pause mid-step when I see a guy put his hands on Quinn's hips. "Mine," I growl, but that anger turns to shock when Quinn moves to the side, and I get a clear look at who she's talking to—the guy she mistook as me when she conceived Tootsie.

QUINN

"HEY," look-alike Hendrix says with a smirk. His eyes are full of hunger, no doubt he's thinking he's in for a repeat of our night together.

"H-h-h-hey," I stammer. My heart is racing as I stare at the man whose baby I'm carrying. At the man I never in a million years thought I would ever see again, but of course, fate is a bitch and here we are. And just when Hendrix and I are good, she throws look-alike Hendrix at me. *Fuck you, fate.*

My eyes widen when I feel the real Hendrix behind me. He places his hands on my hips just where look-alike

Hendrix's were, but this time, my skin tingles and my whole body sparks to life. Just like it always does, and that feeling of stupidity from my night with look-alike slams into me once again because I should have known he wasn't *my* Hendrix.

Knowing I need to tell him about the baby, I lean into him. "Can we talk for a moment?"

He nods and takes my hand in his. Hendrix growls at this, and he immediately drops my hand. Closing my eyes, I take a deep breath, and then we follow look-alike Hendrix as he leads us to a quieter spot to chat. We walk toward the back of the club and down a dark corridor. If this was a horror movie, I'd think I was being led to my death and in a way, it kinda feels like I am.

Hendrix slides his hand into mine, lacing our fingers together, and knowing he's here with me makes this a little less nerve-wracking.

"What's up?" look-alike Hendrix says after a few beats of silence. His eyes drop to my and Hendrix's joined hands and he begins to nod.

"Jim," he says to Hendrix, offering his hand.

Hendrix surprises me when he drops my hand, takes Jim's, and shakes. "Hendrix." He doesn't puff out his chest like I thought he might. Instead, he shows Jim and me respect, and that makes me all gooey for him that much more than if he went all alpha and punched Jim.

The three of us fall silent and when it becomes deafening, I speak, well, I try to speak. "So, umm …" I fumble with my words due to the nerves coursing through my veins. Hendrix laces our fingers together again and squeezes, giving me a boost of strength to confess all to Jim, but then the alpha asshole asserts his dominance when he shuffles behind me and rests his hand on my bump.

Jim's gaze drops to Hendrix's hands, his eyes widen, and he nods.

"Argh, I see, you're taken and …"

"No, um, well yes, I'm with Hendrix, but I'm pregnant and it's yours."

"Yeah. Nah, not possible," he says with a chuckle, and my heart drops at him dismissing me and his baby so easily. "It's not mine," he adds, causing my heart to constrict further when I hear him dismiss me and the baby.

"Look, you don't need to do anything. I … I just wanted you to know."

His gaze flicks between Hendrix, me, and my belly, then he laughs and it pisses me off, again.

"Can't be mine, his maybe, but definitely not mine."

"But the timing …" I say, pleading with him. "You're the father." It has to be his, I haven't slept with anyone else.

"Look, Quinn, I'd own up to it for sure if it was mine." I roll my eyes because he's full of shit. "Seriously, I would, but there is no way that baby is mine. I had an accident when I was little. It, umm, ahh, it left me sterile. I can never have kids, Quinn. Ever."

Huh? "Wait, what?" I'm so confused right now. "You're sterile?"

He nods. "It's not mine, Quinn. Maybe you slept with someone else around the same time?" He steps into me and kisses my cheek. "Good luck and I hope you find the father."

My face falls as I stand here and watch him walk away. My heart sinks because the baby daddy just walked away from me. Hendrix pulls me into his chest, hugs me from behind, and kisses my ear.

"It doesn't matter, baby, I told you, I'm all in," Hendrix says, reassuring me he'll be here for us. Closing my eyes, I lean back into him. He slides his hand over my bump and my eyes fly open. My body stiffens when it hits me.

The only guy I slept with is currently holding me in his arms.

A smile appears on my face because it means Hendrix IS the father. Seems I'm further along in my pregnancy than we think—damn you, polycystic ovaries and an irregular period cycle, making this harder than it had to be. With that knowledge, I feel lighter and now I have to find the perfect way to tell him he *is* my baby daddy.

HENDRIX

WATCHING THAT GUY WALK AWAY, my heart drops for Quinn. She was positive the guy who eerily looks like me was the dad but if it's not him, who is it? She stiffens in my arms and quickly spins to face me. Her smile is wide and not what I expected to see.

"Quinn, you okay?"

She nods and then presses her lips to mine. She kisses me deeply, and I find myself kissing her back. I slide my hands into her luscious locks and gently tug. Pulling on the strands, I earn myself a moan that has my cock coming to life between us.

"I need to fuck you," I tell her when she pulls back. She looks nervous and shakes her head. "You don't want to fuck?" Again, a headshake. "Are you sick?" I question because Quinn never turns me down and especially not since she became pregnant.

"I ... I need to tell you something, but I can't do it now. Can you wait for me?"

She bites her lip, waiting for my reply. Lifting my hand, I pull her glossy lip free of her teeth and run the pad of my finger over the indents. "Quinn, just tell me 'cause to be honest, you're starting to scare me."

"Not now, but soon."

I can't read her right now and I don't know if I should be scared or excited. Whatever the case, I guess I need to bide my time until she's ready to tell me whatever it is. "You know you can tell me anything, Quinn, and whatever you have to tell me, tell me in your own time. Now, let's go rejoin our friends."

She nods again but she looks uneasy. Reaching out, I take her hands in mine and squeeze, reassuring her that whatever she has to tell me will be all good. I'm already stepping in to play dad, what else could there be?

"You two look freshly fucked," Saint says, slapping me on the back as we rejoin them. Quinn takes a seat on my lap, and my hands find their way to her bump.

"That will come later," I tell him with a wink.

"You dirty dog, you," Saint says, offering me his fist and earning himself an eye roll from Rowan.

"Dude, I just saw a guy who looked eerily like you," Hudson says, passing me one of the beers he just placed on the table between us, and a mineral water to Quinn.

"That's Jim," I tell them.

"You know him?"

"Kinda. Sorta. Not really, but forget about look-alike me, let's celebrate."

A chorus of congratulations for Lauren filters around the group but the moment is broken when a girl walks up to us. She hugs Lauren tightly and apologizes for being late. Then she pulls Quinn from my lap and hugs her. Quinn stands next to the newcomer, and the longer I stare at her, the more familiar she looks, but I don't think I've ever seen her before. Then she speaks and everyone's mouths drop in shock.

RISA

"HI, I'M RISA," I say when I finally get to the club. My parents wanted to celebrate with me first, and I cannot say no to them. But I'm here now and it's time to get the party started.

Everyone's mouths drop open, and a guy pushes his chair back violently, tipping it over. He turns to face me, and as soon as I get a good look at him, I furrow my brows. He looks familiar, but I guarantee I have never met him. The more I look at his face, the more I notice we look similar. We have the same shaped nose, and our eyes are the same shade of green, but I swear I have never seen him before.

"Wwwwwhat did you say your name was?" he stammers, walking closer to me.

"Risa," I tell him as I offer him my hand. "And you are?"

He swallows, his Adam's apple sliding down his throat as he does. "Rian, my name is Rian."

"Holy fucking shit," someone breathes.

He runs his hands through his hair, the strands stick up in all kinds of places, and that's when I notice our hair color is the same too.

"Ri," Lauren says, and we both look toward her. She's giving me a weird look, but before I can look back to this Rian person again, he returns to his seat and rejoins his friends. Lauren pulls me to the side. "Are you okay?" she asks.

Nodding, I smile at my friend. "Yeah, fine, but I think I know that guy." She nods too but doesn't say anything, and I get this sixth sense that whatever drama is about to unfold, here isn't the time or place for it to happen.

Lauren goes back to her chair, and I take a seat at the table. The only one left is next to this Rian person. *Of course it is.* He eyes me casually as I wait for the hostess to return so I can order a drink.

"I feel like I know you," he murmurs, startling me. "But that's impossible because this is the first time we're meeting. Right?"

Again, I nod. I'm starting to feel like one of those bobblehead dolls. But he's right, I feel like I know him. There's this weird pull between us but it's not sexual, it's platonic.

"This is weird right?" He chuckles, and I can't help but laugh too.

"Fuck, this is so messed up," he says, sipping his drink.

"Can we get breakfast in the morning?" I ask out of nowhere. The urge to get to know him is strong, and I know it'll be better to talk one-on-one and without the loud music and a crowd behind us.

"I'd like that," Rian agrees, and I can't help but smile.

Why am I excited for breakfast with this stranger?

Rian and I chat through the night, getting to know each other, and the more I find out about him, the more this connection of sorts grows.

At the end of the night, we all say our goodbyes and we agree to meet tomorrow at my favorite café. Something strange is going on, and I need to get to the bottom of this.

My leg bounces nervously while I wait for Rian. I'm on coffee number two when I start to think he's stood me up, but I look up and see him walking toward me. He waves when he sees me and just like last night, that feeling of knowing him slams into me.

"Hey," he says, kissing my cheek and taking a seat across from me.

"Hey," I nervously reply.

"So, I recently found out I'm adopted," Rian states. Seems we're getting right into this.

"I'm adopted, too," I tell him. His eyes widen when I tell him this. "My parents are great," I add, feeling the need to defend them.

"My parents are great too, and I'm glad I have them, but when I found out I was adopted, I also found out I had a sister."

My mouth drops open. "Oh my God," slips out. "Is it weird I'm feeling a connection to you? Not in a sexual way, it's … I can't pinpoint what it is, but there's something there."

He nods "I feel it too but, umm, there's more," he says. "The adoption papers I found, they said my sister's name is, yours."

"What?" It comes out like a hiss and I didn't mean it too sound the way it did.

"My, umm, my sister, her name is Risa."

"Oh." My head moves up and down as I process all of this. So that's why they were all shocked when I said my name last night. "Do you think we could be brother and sister?" I ask him.

He sighs, raking his fingers through his hair. "Look, I don't know what to think anymore. I just want to find my sister. Risa is a unique name, and maybe I'm wrong about it being you, but …" He drifts off.

Reaching out, I cover his hand with mine and I smile over at him. "We can always take a test, you know, to find out." He nods. After agreeing to each get tested, we put aside all thoughts of adoptions and us being related and we enjoy breakfast together.

A few hours later, we say our goodbyes after swapping numbers and I head home.

After putting a load of wash in, I dial my parents' number. "Hey, baby," Mom says, and I can hear her smile through the phone.

"Mom?"

"Yes, Risa, baby."

"Do I have a brother?"

"Oh," she says, shocked at my question. "I'm not sure, darling. I mean, it's possible. Why do you ask?"

"I met this guy at the club last night, and Mom, we look eerily similar, and I felt this instant connection with him. Is that weird?" I ask her, knowing she'll always be honest with me.

"No, baby, that's not weird at all. Leave it with me. Your father and I will look into it but remember, we love you."

"Love you too, Mom." I hang up feeling somewhat lighter. But what if Rian is my brother? I've always wanted a sibling, but knowing my parents could never have children and adoption was expensive, I never pushed it. They chose to adopt me, and I was so lucky they did because Felix and Penelope Davenport are the best parents a girl could ask for. But since meeting Rian last night, I have so many questions. What if it's just a coincidence? I mean, this is too good to be true, right?

God, I hope this doesn't turn into some big mess and it all implodes. The last thing I want is to drag some random guy into a messy situation, but what if we are?

I hope my parents find something, and I hope they find something soon, because if Rian is my brother, I want to get to know him.

HENÐRIX

AS IF I don't have enough on my plate. When we returned from New York, Rian went off the rails and then MIA. There's a huge chance Risa is his sister. Mother refuses to tell us what went down when she, Aunt Tamsyn, and Uncle Michael spoke to the family lawyer, Mr. Ellis. All she keeps saying is all will be revealed as and when it's meant to be, and we just need to be there for our cousin.

On top of all that shit, Quinn's been acting weird. Ever since we got back from New York, she's been distant. It's almost as if she can't stand to be in the same room as me.

That the thought of me touching her will give her cooties or boy germs. It's been three days and I've had enough.

Storming into the girls' bathroom, the door flies open and bounces back into me as I march in. "Hendrix," Remy screams, covering herself. "What the fuck, dude?"

Ignoring her, I head straight for Quinn, knowing which shower she's in since she uses the same one every damn time.

Pulling the curtain back, Quinn screams until she realizes it's me. "Hendrix, what the hell?" she breathes, covering her chest. My eyes rake over her bubble covered chest and my dick twitches, but then I remember she's being a bitch and I shake that thought away.

"We need to talk," I demand.

"It couldn't wait?" she snaps the question at me as she reaches behind me and closes the curtain. She steps back under the spray and continues to rinse off.

"No," I deadpan and cross my arms.

Quinn being Quinn, she finishes rinsing her hair and then turns the water off. She steps out and wraps one of her fucking hideous orange towels around her body.

Then she stands there with her hands on her hips, waiting for me to speak but now that the floor is mine, I'm suddenly nervous.

"Are you leaving me for him?" I dejectedly ask her. I know I'm being irrational right now. Jim all but wiped his hands but I'm haven't found out who the father is. Maybe she's going to run off with him, whoever he may be and play happy family without me.

Quinn's eyes widen and she gawks at me. Her mouth opens and closes, unsure of what to say. I've caught her off-guard but her nonanswer is answer enough.

Running my hands through my hair, I pull on the

strands and shake my head. "I fucking knew it," I scoff, my heart breaking at the realization I've lost her. I go to storm away, but Quinn's fingers wrap around my bicep and her touch instantly calms me. When I look back over my shoulder, the look in her face forces me to stay.

She stares at me but does not utter a word, so I say what I feel. "I was all fucking in, Quinn. Even though that kid wasn't fucking mine, I stepped up. I love you and Tootsie, and now, now you want to head off with that fucker. I just …"

Quinn grabs my face in her palms and kisses me. Wrapping her arms around my neck, she stands on her tiptoes and pushes her tongue into my mouth. Kissing me passionately to shut me up.

My hands find her ass and I squeeze hard. Tapping her towel covered cheeks, she jumps up into my arms and stares at me.

"I'm scared … and confused, Hendrix," she tells me, her eyes welling with tears.

"What the fuck for?" I growl.

"Because it all became real and then when he told me he wasn't the father because it's impossible, I knew who was, and it just made it all so real."

Great, another fucker I have to compete with.

"Okay, fine, so you fucked someone else."

Quinn wipes a stray tear falling down her cheek.

"Hendrix, I …" she whispers.

"Un-fucking-believable, Quinn. You slept with two dudes? What the ever-loving fuck!"

Knowing Quinn slept with that dipshit in New York was one thing, but she fucked someone else too? Fucking hell, I'm so stupid. Why did it take me a few days to realize this? And why didn't she tell me she slept with someone else? I thought we were past the lies and manip-ulation. Unceremoniously, I drop her to her feet and turn my back on her.

Pulling the curtain open, I walk away from her. More hurt than ever before. Quinn calls after me as I leave the bathroom, but my anger is at boiling point, and I don't trust myself right now. Slamming the door behind me, I race back to the boys' floor, passing my brother along the way.

Saint stops when I walk past him, and he calls out to me, but again, I don't want to hit someone I care about so I ignore him.

"Hendrix," he yells, but again, I continue to ignore him. I storm down the stairs and out the front door with him hot on my tail. I'm about to round the corner when I run into Reign and Hudson carrying Rian, who's mumbling loudly to himself.

"What the fuck?" Saint and I say at the same time.

"We just found him like this," Hudson says, trying to hold up Rian.

"Fuck's sake, I thought we were done with this shit?" I sigh.

Putting my messed-up life aside, I help them lift Rian so he doesn't face plant on the ground. "Let's get him upstairs. Saint, call Thatch."

Helping Reign and Hudson carry Rian is a difficult task. The fucker weighs a ton at the best of times, but drunk, he's a dead fucking weight.

After a few struggles and near mishaps of dropping him, we finally get to Thatcher's room. He's standing in the doorway, waiting for us.

"Lie him down." Thatcher growls. Whatever is going on with Rian has us all worried.

Rian mumbles again and Reign leans down, trying to work out what he's rambling about. Giving us all confused looks, Reign chuckles.

"Um, there is no way what he just said is true," Reign retorts, looking at Hudson who seems to have heard it too.

"What did he say?" Saint asks.

"He said you guys are such good brothers," Reign murmurs.

What the fuck.

QUINN

I'VE BEEN AVOIDING HENDRIX. Okay, well, not avoiding him but things between us have been awkward since we got back from New York and I realized what I did about Tootsie. Hendrix thinks I'm leaving him for Jim. As if any guy would and could ever compare to the real Hendrix Vanderbelt.

After him storming out of the bathrooms last night, he was occupied with more Rian crap, but when I woke up this morning, I decided that today is the day. Today is the day I tell Hendrix what I always wanted to be true. He's the father, this baby—our baby—is his.

Putting together the final pieces of my surprise, a loud bang sounds on my door followed by a voice I'd recognize anywhere growling, "Quinn, open this door right fucking now."

I smile at how assertive Hendrix sounds on the other side. Fixing my outfit, I reach for the handle and open the door, and before I can say anything, Hendrix barges straight in rambling before I get a word in.

"I don't give a fuck about anything. I'm done with you avoiding me, and I don't care who the daddy is. I will pummel any guy's face in if it means you're mine because you are. You and Tootsie are mine."

When he finally stops with his rant, I hold out the small box I put together for him.

"What's this?" he asks.

"Open it," I say, handing it to him.

He slowly takes a seat on the edge of my bed, his fingers quickly unwrapping the small bow I fastened on top. I watch him as he lifts the lid, throwing it to the floor. He rummages through the tissue paper and stops when he gets to the gift.

Staring at the small onesie inside, he slowly pulls it from the box and reads what's printed on it. I watch the way his face pales, knowing he's reading the words I had sewed on to it. He swallows and a single tear slides down his cheek before he looks at me.

Grasping the onesie between his fingers, Hendrix lets out the breath he was holding and drops down on to the corner of my bed. He reaches out and I place my hand in his. He pulls me onto his lap and crashes his lips to mine in an all-consuming kiss that leaves me breathless and panting with need.

Breaking the kiss, his eyes flick between the box and me, and he finally asks, "Is this what I think it is?"

HENDRIX

"IT IS," she tells me.

"How? Why? I'm so confused."

"Okay, so, umm, that guy who I thought was Tootsie's father told us he wasn't when we were in New York, so that only leaves one other person as the daddy and that, umm, means you'rethebabydaddy." She says the last four words quickly, but I hear them clear as day.

Blinking a few times, I process her words and then look back at the onesie, and it sinks in it's me.

I'm

The

Daddy

Quinn stares intently at me, she still looks like she's going to throw up and with her being pregnant, that's highly possible.

Lifting my hands, I cup her cheeks in my palms. "Say that again?" I demand, my tone harsher than I intended and she recoils into herself. "Quinn, say that last part again … please?"

"Tootsie is yours, Hendrix. You're the father."

Staring at her, I repeatedly play those words over in my head.

You're the father.

I'm the father.

Tootsie is mine.

"I'm the dad," I voice, and Quinn nods. "That baby in your belly isn't that guy's or some other fucker's, she's mine." Again she nods.

"Tootsie is yours," Quinn tearfully mumbles. "She's yours."

Pulling her into me, I once again cover her mouth with mine, and against her lips, I whisper, "I'm going to be a dad."

"You're going to be a dad," she repeats, resting her forehead against mine.

A smile breaks out on my face. Lifting her off my lap, I drop to my knees in front of her and place my hands on her bump. "Hey, Tootsie, I was already your dad, but it seems I really am your dad. I'm going to love you so much and spoil you and be there for you. You will know uncon-ditional love and one day, I'm going to marry your mom and give you another brother or sister."

"Hendrix," Quinn cries from above. She drops to her knees before me and grips my cheeks in her palms. "I love you so so much. Hendrix. I'm so fucking happy you're the daddy and I'm so so sorry I thought you weren't."

"Babe, I always was the daddy, DNA or not."

QUINN

"BABE, I always was the daddy, DNA or not." Those words mean everything to me and my love for him blooms even further, especially when he adds, "I fucking love you, Quinn Ellis. So fucking much."

He slams his lips to mine and kisses me before I can reply.

Holding his face between my hands, I kiss him back, moaning around him as he deepens the kiss. He climbs back onto my bed, and I straddle him as we continue to kiss. His cock hardens under me and my pussy clenches. Hendrix groans and lifts me up to free his cock. He bunches my dress around my waist and moves my panties to the side. Gripping his dick, he guides the head to my slit and thrusts inside me in one move. Forcing us both to groan out loud.

"Fuck, your pussy gets better every fucking time," Hendrix hisses through clenched teeth. Placing his hands under my ass, he moves me up and down over his cock, while his teeth find my skin, biting down and leaving a mark on my shoulder. Moaning, my arms wrap around his neck while he fucks wildly, his cock throbbing inside me. Grunting, Hendrix slams me down over his cock. My pussy clenches down on his cock while my body shakes violently with a wave of pleasure only he can pull from me.

Hendrix curses and then he's filling me up, holding me down. Both of us panting and gripping onto each other tightly as we come down from our high.

I begin to giggle.

"What's so funny?" Hendrix smiles.

"I just love us, you know." Feeling a sudden sweep of emotion, I can't help the tear that slides down my face.

"Hey," Hendrix says, gripping my face between his hands. "I fucking love you, Quinn. I already told you I'm all in, baby. All. Fucking. In."

We snuggle in my bed together, just holding one another. "Fuck, I can't believe it," Hendrix says, his hand spreading over my belly. Looking down at me, his gaze lingers with one of those perfect smiles he wears.

"I'm glad Tootsie is yours, Hendrix. I'm so sorry I messed up and …"

"Shh," he tells me, placing his finger against my lips. "It doesn't matter because I'm going to be a daddy." He smiles, his eyes lighting up when he says the words out loud.

"And we're still not going to find out what it is, right?" he says.

"Of course." I smile.

"Fuck," he says, a look of despair on his face.

"What?"

"What if it's a boy?" He sighs. "Fuck, what if he's just like me and my brothers, fuck. Or, what if it's a girl and she falls for someone like me?" I begin to giggle. "This isn't funny, Quinn."

His worry is perfect, and to lessen his fear I just kiss him, knowing he'll stress himself out if I don't shut him up now.

"You're going to be the best daddy, Hendrix."

"I love you," he mutters, kissing me once more before moving over the top of me and kissing me again.

I whisper, "We love you too."

And together we show each other just how much we love each other for the rest of the day. We stay in our blissful bubble, happy and content, but I know our little bubble won't last forever because we live in Crestwood and it's never smooth sailing for long in this place.

HENDRIX

"WE HAVE NEWS," I announce at the cafeteria later that day when we join everyone for an early dinner. Everyone stops what they are doing and looks intently at us. Thatch even pauses mid-spoonful, dropping some carbonara onto his shirt.

"I'm going to be a dad," I proudly declare to the group. They all silently stare at me.

"No shit," Rian scoffs, dropping his gaze to Quinn's bump. "That's old news."

"No, I'm actually the dad," I tell them again, and you

can't stop the smile on my face. Ever since Quinn dropped the bomb that Tootsie is mine, I've been happier than I ever have been before. I was excited to help Quinn, but now, that excitement has ramped up to an 'I'm going to Disneyland' level of excitement.

"Huh?" Rian deadpans. "What do you mean?" Looking around at everyone, they all have that blank 'huh' look too.

"Well, Quinn thought someone else was the dad, but I stepped up, 'cause well, she's Quinn and I'm awesome like that." Someone scoffs, probably Saint, but I ignore him and continue, "I couldn't leave her in the lurch and stepped up, but when we were in New York the other week, she spoke with him."

"The dude who looked like you?" Hudson asks.

Nodding, I continue, "Well, it turns out he's shooting blanks so that only left me, and now, I'm officially the daddy even though I was already the daddy."

Everyone just sits there, blinking at Quinn and I. Processing what I just word-vomited. Thatch drops his fork, slams the table, pushes himself up into a standing position, and walks over to us. "Congrats, guys. So happy for you both." He pulls Quinn into a hug, and I watch him embrace her. Then he turns to me and pulls me in as well. Slapping my back in the bro kind of way, he whispers, "You are going to make an amazing dad, Hendrix."

"And you'll be an amazing uncle," I tell him.

"We *all* will make amazing uncles," Saint says, joining us with Reign and Hudson close behind him.

More bro hugs are thrown around and then it's the girls' turn. They all gush over how amazing I am, and I can't help but push my chest out a little. I didn't step up for the accolade of doing the right thing. I stepped up because Quinn needed help and I'm not an asshole. Well, most of the time I'm not.

"This calls for a celebration," Thatch declares. He jumps up onto the table and announces to the cafeteria, "Party tonight in the cemetery. We are celebrating Hendrix being a dad and the upcoming arrival of my niece or nephew, Tootsie."

A chorus of cheers and applause echoes around the room.

Looks like we have a party to attend.

"Parties suck donkey dick when you can't drink," Quinn complains as I pull her onto my lap after refilling my beer. I pause with my Solo cup halfway to my lips and suddenly feel bad that I'm drinking. Tossing the liquid in my cup out, I throw the empty cup into the fire and pull her in closer. I nuzzle her neck before biting on her earlobe, then whisper, "I know something we can do that doesn't need alcohol. We just need your pretty pussy and my dick." She looks at me over her shoulder, and with the glow of the fire behind her she looks stunning. "You look fucking gorgeous tonight," I blurt out.

"I'm fat and puffy and really really want a vodka, lime, and soda right now."

"You're pregnant, therefore not fat and puffy. You can have a lime and soda, sans vodka but in a few short months, I will feed you all the vodka, lime, and sodas you want. I'll even hold your hair back when you vomit."

"And they say romance is dead," she says with an eye

roll. "But I don't think there will be many vodka, lime, and sodas in my future 'cause we will have a baby to look after and I can only guess that a hangover with a screaming baby will suck donkey dick."

"Well, the offer is there … on both accounts."

"Can we really sneak out of a party that's in our honor to fuck?"

"We can do whatever the fuck we want, Quinn." She stares at me and the look in her eyes tells me everything. "So, what's it going to be, baby? Party or fuck?"

"I think you know, Hendrix. I think you know."

She stares at me, and the air around us thickens with desire, much like my dick, but I want her to tell me what she wants. "I'm gonna need you to spell it out for me."

"I want you to take me back to my room …"

"And once we get there?"

She stands up and straddles my lap, draping her arms over my shoulders. She stares deep into my soul and begins to tell me what she wants. "As soon as my door clicks closed, you are going to remove your clothes and I'm going to remove mine, leaving us both naked as the day we were born."

"And once we're both naked?"

"I'm going to eye-fuck you 'cause you, Hendrix Vanderbelt, are a masterpiece. Then I'm going to drop to my knees and suck your dick like it's a popsicle melting on a hot summer's day until you come down my throat."

My cock twitches between us. Just the thought of her lips wrapped around my shaft has me ready to come, and she hasn't even touched me. "And after I've come?"

"You're going to help me up to my feet 'cause I'm fat and puffy and can't do that on my own anymore. Once I'm standing, it'll be your turn to eye-fuck me. I want to feel your gaze slide over my body. I want my skin to tingle as your eyes roam from my tits to my pussy and when you reach my eyes again, you're going to grip my cheeks in your palms and you're going to kiss me."

Not able to stop myself, I grip her cheeks in my hands and cover her mouth with mine. My tongue slides into her mouth and hers slides into mine. She runs her fingernails up into my hair, and I moan into the kiss. "I fucking love kissing you."

"I love you in general," she mumbles against my lips, "but when you kiss me in my room, you're going to taste yourself on my lips."

"I can't fucking wait, we should get out of here." It's phrased as a statement, not a question but she shakes her head.

"I want to finish telling you what's going to happen when we get back to my room."

"By all means, the floor is yours."

"Okay, so you're kissing me after I've blown you. While we're kissing, you will back me into my room door and keep kissing me while you play with my boobs."

"And what will happen after you are pressed against the door and your tits are mashed into my chest?"

"I didn't say anything about my tits and your chest."

"I went off script because after playing with your tits, my chest wanted to feel the tight, taut peaks of your nipples pressed into it."

"I will allow that amendment, but after the tits mashing, you will drop to your knees before me. You will lift one of my legs over your shoulder, and then you are going to lick, suck, and finger me until I'm screaming your name for all on the floor to hear. My hands are going to press your face so tight into my pussy that you might suffocate."

"I'm happy to oblige on all accounts and let me just say, suffocation by your cunt would be a wonderful way to die. So, after you've finished screaming my name and I don't die from cuntfication, what will happen next?"

"You will lower my leg and stand up. You will kiss me so I can taste myself on your lips. After we make out and your dick is poking me in the stomach, you will escort me over to the bed. You will lie down on your back, and once you are comfy, I will climb on top of you. I will sink down on your dick until I'm fully seated and your dick is deep inside me. I will begin to ride you and you will massage my clit and my tits. Pulling on my nipples and rolling the tips between your thumb and forefinger and—"

"This is so fucking hot, Quinn, I'm ready to come and we are both fully clothed and surrounded by our family and friends."

"Well, let me finish story time, and then we can make it become a reality."

"Deal ... now continue. You're riding me, and I'm fondling your tits and playing with your clit."

"Okay, so, you're fondling and playing with me. Meanwhile, I'm riding you like a pro bull rider and then we will come together. Moaning each other's names as we succumb to the pleasure."

"And once we've both come?"

"You will go and get a wet cloth and clean us both up. Then we'll snuggle under the covers, naked, and we will fall asleep in each other's arms. Our fingers entwined and resting on Tootsie."

"That's quite the scene and I say we leave and make it come true."

And make it come true we do, and let me tell you, story time was hot but in real life, holy fucking hotness. If I didn't already love Quinn with all my heart and soul, after that session, I was gaga for her.

I'm one lucky son of a bitch, and one day, I'm going to make my baby momma my wife.

RIAN

I'VE BEEN GOING FUCKING crazy. The only thing keeping me somewhat sane is whatever cheap liquor I can get my hands on and my cousins, who as it turns out, are NOT my brothers. They have been my lifeline since my world imploded, and it seems the implosions just keep coming. I know I can't keep doing this, especially to my parents.

Parents, plural.

Tamsyn and Michael Vanderbelt are my parents. A

little background on my parents, they are hopelessly in love with one another, it's sickening at times. Get this, my dad was so gaga for my mom that he took her last name when they married and when it comes down to it, it's just a name. But I will admit, having the last name of Vander-belt around here gets you things that most eighteen-year-olds only dream of. We may not share DNA, but they have been there for me from pretty much the moment I was born. End of story. That's all a kid wants, unconditional love, and that's exactly what I have had my whole life. Yes, they were there for me when I was only a few days old and have been there for me ever since, but their love was covering a lie and I can't get past that.

Nerves are fluttering about my body right now because today we are catching up with my sister and her parents. The blood tests we had when I got back from New York confirmed last week that Risa and I are related. I have a sister, and not just a sister but a twin sister.

Fuck, I'm a twin.

My entire life, I'd always wanted a sibling, and now I have a sister and a whole other family.

In the last few weeks since finding my sister, they have really stepped up. As have Risa's parents. It's a comfort knowing she was adopted into a good family. Mr. and Mrs. Davenport seem like good people, from what I know so far. What with all the messed-up shit Uncle Thornton was involved in, it could have been bad for her but, thankfully, she ended up with two loving parents.

She's coming here to Crestwood today to meet the extended family. After running into her in New York the other week, I've been on edge. One chance encounter in The Big Apple, and I find my sister. What are the fucking chances of that?

My parents are out front with Aunt Estelle, waiting for the Davenports to arrive. My leg is bouncing with nerves, and I'm trying my best to calm myself without alcohol or weed. Taking a deep breath, I drop my head back and stare up at the ceiling.

Hendrix takes a seat next to me, slapping my thigh. "Dude, it's all going to work out," he tells me, but how the fuck does he know that?

"I know, it's just nerve-wracking. My life has been a fucking roller coaster these past few months with finding out I'm adopted and then randomly bumping into my sister, in a bar of all places. I just, fuck, I'm so nervous. What if she hates me? What if ..."

"You guys are twins, and take it from us," Saint says, nodding at Hendrix and Thatcher, "that's a bond that you cannot break or fake. I saw the two of you that night in New York, there's a connection there. With time, you will be the bestest of friends, who at times want to stab the other with a fork, but for the most part, they are your person, and when you are with them, everything is right in the world."

Chuckling at my cousin's assessment, I smile. I pray he's right, but deep down I already know he is. My cousins' triplet bond is like nothing else I've witnessed, but will that happen for me and Risa too? I really want that with my twin, and maybe now, I will have someone to confide in. Someone I can tell my deepest darkest secrets to. I need that because I have a secret I've been keeping from everyone. Something I'm too afraid to say out loud, but before I can dwell on my secret anymore, Reign arrives, followed by Thatcher and my parents.

"Honey," my mother's voice echoes across the room,

and with that one word from my mom, my nerves dissipate, and I somehow know it's all going to be okay.

Pushing myself up, I awkwardly stand and wait. Dad steps in behind Mom and stops before ushering in my sister, she's a petite blond girl who looks so much like me. Behind her is another couple who I recognize as Risa's parents, Felix and Penelope. She looks nervous, which is somehow comforting, and when our gazes meet, I instantly feel whole.

How the fuck does that happen?

One look across a room, and that missing piece of me is suddenly filled. Her gaze crosses mine, and she gives me a soft smile. In sync, we both cross into the middle of the room and stop inches apart. It feels like the air has been taken from the room, but at the same time, it's filled with something that envelops us and cements this is where we are meant to be, and I know everything is going to work out just fine.

RISA

I'M SO NERVOUS, my entire body shakes as we drive toward the house. Toward my cousins' house, and my brother.

It's still surreal that I have a brother and a whole family I knew nothing about.

Finding out I was adopted was a shock. I always thought I looked just like my mom, but we don't even share the same DNA. They swear they didn't know about Rian, but there's a small amount of doubt in my mind that they knew about him. I don't know why I doubt them, I mean, they never kept my adoption a secret, why would they lie about my twin? When Mom looks back at me and smiles, I see nothing but love reflecting back at me, and I know they didn't keep him from me. Then I feel like a bitch for thinking they kept Rian a secret.

Dad turns off the main road and starts driving up a long driveway. "We aren't in Kansas anymore, Toto," I mumble to myself as he pulls into the turning circle and stops the car. He looks at me through the rearview mirror. "You good, kiddo?" he asks. His jaw ticks like he's holding back. Finding out I was a twin was a complete shock to all of us. All these years, I had a brother, a twin, out there. A male version of me was walking around and we were none the wiser.

One night, I overheard Mom and Dad talking in hushed tones. They were saying they felt bad they didn't know about Rian and should have done it properly, whatever that means.

"Let's go, Dad." I give him a smile so he knows I'm okay. He and Mom have been worried about me nonstop, hovering like helicopter parents. I know they mean well but I'm eighteen and I'm fine. My parents climb out and I take a few seconds of alone time to take some much-needed deep breaths.

I'm starting to freak out.

I'm about to officially meet my brother. Yes, we met the other week in New York, but this is different. We now have a piece of paper confirming we're related. It somehow feels different, almost official.

My parents even offered to uproot our lives in New York and move to Crestwood and enroll me at Crestwood Prep next semester so I'm closer to my brother, but I told them I wanted to stay in New York because I belong at Stepz. Dancing on Broadway has been my dream from the moment I walked into Miss Maisie's dance studio when I was five.

Dad opens my door, and my moment of solitude is gone. He offers me his hand and I place mine in his, and hand in hand with my mom on my other side, we make our way up the front steps and knock.

A few moments later, a lady opens the door. She says she's Lisette and gestures for us to enter. Her soft smile is oddly comforting, making me slightly less nervous to be in this big fancy house.

"This way, please." She smiles, turns, and waits for us to follow her.

With small steps, we follow Lisette farther into the house. Tamsyn and Michael, Rian's parents step out of a room and greet us. Awkward hellos are swapped, and then they usher us into another room. The door lays open, waiting for us. His parents step in, and then myself and my parents follow. I feel him before I see him, twin intuition or something else, I'm not sure. Tamsyn says, "Honey." He looks toward her, and I step out from behind his mom, but the moment I see him, every puzzle piece connects, making me feel whole.

He stands up from where he was sitting and like the first time I saw him, I take in his height. He's tall, much taller than me, and his blond shaggy hair curls over his forehead, making him look like a member of a nineties boy band. In the daylight, I notice his lip is pierced, matching my nose ring. His throat bobs when he swallows and seeing him as nervous as me makes me smile.

Stepping toward me, he stops and nervously says, "I'm Rian."

"Risa," I reply and giggle. "But we already know that." He chuckles too and then holds his hand out. My hand slips into his, and then he pulls me into his arms, enclosing me in a hug. I slowly wrap my arms around his waist, resting my head on his shoulder. I close my eyes and take the moment in. This is my first hug with my twin. It's difficult because he's at least a head and a bit taller than me, but somehow, we fit together.

Towering over me, I lift my head and look up at him. "Hi," I whisper.

"Hi," he murmurs softly.

RIAN

MY SISTER and I silently hug one another and then my parents join us. They wrap their arms around Risa and me. My mother's soft tears filter around us and her quiet sobs are the only thing I can hear. Then another set of arms joins us, and I see Mr. and Mrs. Davenport, Risa's parents, have joined our group hug.

"I can't believe it," Mom mutters, breaking the hug circle. She grips both our hands and stares at me and Risa. Risa's mom sidles up to my mom and her gaze flicks between us as well, tears welling in her eyes.

"Your resemblance is remarkable. Even without the DNA test, you can tell you two are related," Mom says.

"Definitely," Penelope replies. "You know, we always wanted a sibling for Risa, but we gave our life savings to Thornton for the adoption, but we never knew you were twins. Had we known, we … we probably couldn't have afforded both of you and as selfish as this is, I'm glad we got Risa. She's the light of our life but, Rian, we'd … we'd like to get to know you too." She pauses. "That's only if you want. We don't want to push or take you from your parents. We just want Risa to feel whole. She always said she was missing something and I think it was you."

"Rian always said the same thing," Mom tells Penelope.

Our reunion is halted when Jack Ellis, Quinn's dad, walks in with Lisette. I was so lost in my sister and her parents, I didn't even hear the doorbell ring.

"Mr. Ellis," Hendrix says, jumping up. "Is everything okay with Quinn?"

He nods. "I think so but I'm, umm, here regarding Rian's and Risa's adoptions."

My father wraps an arm around my mother tightly, and I swear his face is pale now. *What does he know?* We all take a seat, and when everyone is sitting, Mr. Ellis begins. "As you are all aware, I'm the one who finalized the adoptions of Rian and Risa at the request of Thornton, and before you ask, I tried to get him to adopt the two of you together, but you know Thornton, what he wants he gets so there were two adoptions instead of one. Both are legally binding, paperwork-wise, but the fundamental elements are less than legal, but that's neither here nor there in the scheme of things."

Mr. Ellis rambles on about legal stuff that I'm pretty

sure none of us give a shit about, and it makes me think he's just covering his ass right now, so I ask the one question that's on the tip of my and everyone's tongue.

"Do you know who our biological parents are?"

He nods but doesn't speak.

"Tell us," my dad demands, and he uses *that* tone that has you almost shitting your pants and answering post haste.

"I swore to Thornton that I would never tell because it was not my secret to share, but he's dead, and I'm not scared of him anymore. You have the right to know."

"Just tell us," I growl at him, earning myself a glare from my mom.

"Tessa Vanderbelt is your biological mother."

The room goes silent as we process the words. I'm a Vanderbelt by blood and my mom's sister is my bio mom. *What the fuck?*

"Tessie," Mom says, covering her mouth and letting out a sob. Tessa Vanderbelt disappeared eighteen years ago, and about six months after she disappeared, a death certificate showed up at our grandfather's. No one knew what happened but, clearly, Thornton and Mr. Ellis knew.

"Start talking, Jack," my dad growls, "now," he tacks on when he remains tight-lipped. There has been no love lost between these two over the years and this betrayal, as such, will be hard for him to forgive.

"From what Thornton said, Tessa was seeing the stable hand—" Mom smiles at this news, it's almost as if she knew and that's confirmed when she interrupts and says as much.

"I used to cover for her and Jordy. They were hopelessly in love, but there was no way Daddy would allow her to marry the stable hand, so they kept their tryst secret."

"It seems she got pregnant and knew she couldn't tell her parents. What would the town think of a Vanderbelt having a baby with someone who works for them? She confided in her big brother, and he helped her."

"Seems Dad wasn't a total cunt after all," Hendrix says, earning himself a slap up the back of the head for his language from Aunt Estelle.

"Hendrix," his mom scolds, "language."

"Anyway," Mr. Ellis continues, ignoring Hendrix's cunt outburst. "He took her away and looked after her throughout her pregnancy. Tessa, unfortunately, died giving birth to you both." Risa gasps and her eyes well with tears. Standing up, I walk over to her and take her hand, offering her comfort over the loss of our mom. "Thornton thought adoption was the best option for you two. For reasons unknown to me, he split you up. I didn't question him because, well, he was a Vanderbelt and you do what they ask. Rian went to Tamsyn and Michael Vanderbelt, and Risa went to Felix and Penelope Davenport. I lodged all the paperwork to make the adoption legal in the eye of the law. Thornton paid someone a lot of money for the papers to disappear. He didn't want anyone to know his baby sister had a child, well, twins, out of wedlock."

"Okay, he's back to cunt status," Hendrix interrupts, earning himself another smack up the back of the head.

"Ohhh, Tessa," my mom mumbles. "I wish I could have been there for you." She wipes at her eyes. "You know, I was so desperate for a baby that when Thornton came to me with one, I didn't question anything. I ... I should have asked questions." Mom looks over to Risa.

"I'm sorry you were split up. I ... I should have done more."

"It's not your fault, Mrs. Vanderbelt," Risa says to Mom.

"Please, call me Tamsyn."

"This isn't your fault. This Thornton person chose to do that, he's the one to be held accountable, but I can't be mad at him. Sounds like he stepped up and was a brother when he needed to be. Does it suck Rian and I missed out on eighteen years together? Yes, but we found each other, and now we have a chance to get to know one another." Risa pauses. "Tamsyn, if it's not too much, I'd love for you to tell me about Tessa one of these days."

"I'd love that," Mom says, smiling at Risa. "You remind me so much of her." Mom turns to me. "You too, Rian. I cannot believe I didn't notice it before now."

"Mr. Ellis," Felix asks, "are you positive the adoptions were legal? Pene and I paid a lot of money for Risa, and I know we went about it the wrong way, but like Tamsyn, we just wanted a baby so much."

"Yes, they are legal. The only illegal part of it was you paying Thornton for Risa. How did you meet him?"

"By chance one day when he was with Tessa. He over-heard Penelope and I saying we'd give anything for a baby, and well, he swooped in and delivered us our dream after we gave him our life savings." He pauses. "I'm sorry you were split up. I feel that if he had not heard us that day, he would have given you both to Tamsyn and Michael. This is—"

"No," Jack voices, interrupting Felix. "He was intent on selling one of them. He needed money for ..." He drifts off and sheepishly looks at Aunt Estelle and she answers for him.

"Rochelle and their illegal dealings together."

"You knew back then?" Thatcher asks his mom. "Why the fuck did you stay?"

"I had triplets and another on the way, I couldn't do it on my own. It was easier to stay, and your father would have taken you all from me, I couldn't let that happen."

"So you stayed and turned to alcohol and pills and still let him have us," Saint snaps. I have never heard him speak like that before, especially to his mom, but like with me the last few weeks, something is going on with him too.

"Saint," Hendrix growls, "lay off Mom. Today is about Risa and Rian reuniting, do not let *him* ruin this for them. Now, let's get Lisette to serve lunch cause I'm fuc … really starving and I'm sure Risa would love to hear stories from your childhood, like the time you loudly and proudly announced, 'My mom thinks my nipples are the cutest!' causing everyone to freeze and look concerned. Then we all burst out laughing when Aunty Tamsyn clarified for everyone, 'DIMPLES. I meant dimples. Rian's dimples are the cutest.'"

"Or the time you farted in gym class and tried to blame your shoe," Thatcher unhelpfully adds.

"Or the time he fart—" Thankfully Dad interrupts Hendrix.

"Leave the boy alone. He can't help that he farts when he's nervous." And Hendrix being Hendrix, makes a fake fart noise.

Everyone bursts out laughing, and we spend the rest of the afternoon together. Sharing stories from our childhood. Aunt Tamsyn and Aunt Estelle tell us some stories about our mom, Tessa. We even got the full story as to why my dad took the Vanderbelt name when he and mom got married. In a nutshell, the Vanderbelts get what they want and for some reason Grandpa wanted it that way. The why will be a secret that he'll take to the grave.

The past few months have been rough, but for the first time since my world imploded, I don't feel so alone anymore. That gaping whole has been filled, I've finally found my place and everything is going to be all right ... for me, at least, because my cousins' world implodes a few weeks later when the secret of all secrets at Crestwood Prep is revealed.

QUINN

"HOLY SHIT, MY DAD KNEW?" Shaking my head, I process all Hendrix just told me. No wonder my dad hated Mr. Vanderbelt but at the same time, what he did for his sister was super sweet ... right up till he split Rian and Risa and took all of her parents' life savings.

"Yep, and that's why he hated everything Vanderbelt."

"Holy shit, that's wild, and now that it's all out in the open, hopefully things between us and him and my mom can get back to normal."

"Here's hoping, but even without this revelation, I

think Tootsie here would have brought us all together. She's a little rock star and she's not even here."

"You know, when you use a pronoun for Tootsie, you say girl."

"I do not, I mix it up," he refutes, but I shake my head.

"Uhh uh, you say she and her ALLLLLLLLL the time. Do you want a little girl?"

"I want a healthy baby, but a little Quinn running around wouldn't be so bad. Better than a little cunt like me."

"You're not a cunt," I tell him, and he gives me the eye. "Okay, you can be at times, but guess what?"

"What?"

"You're my cunt, and *my* cunt would really like your dick to slide into it before we have to go see the doctor."

"I'm sure that can be arranged."

And arrange he does.

Hendrix fucks my cunt hard and we are almost late for my appointment.

"And you're sure you want to find out?" the doctor asks because we've always reiterated that we do not want to find out.

Hendrix answers, "Yes," and I say, "No."

We look at each other and burst out laughing. "I don't want to," I quickly tell him before he gets a word in. "There are very few surprises in life, and I think I want this one to be a surprise."

"Babe, I'm a Vanderbelt, surprise is our family's motto.

But if you want to wait, then we can wait. As I said earlier today, I just want Tootsie to be healthy."

"Are you sure?" I ask him.

"Totally sure and to make it up to me, you can give me a blow job on the way home."

"And on that note, I will finish this up and see you both in a few weeks for the next scan," my doctor says.

Without another word, the doctor wipes down my belly, turns the ultrasound machine off, and hightails it out of the room, leaving me alone with Hendrix. He always manages to make her feel uncomfortable and if he scares her off before Tootsie arrives, I will kill him. She is so calming and nurturing and I'm glad to have her on Team Tootsie

"I think you embarrassed her," Hendrix says.

"Ummm, you're the one who demanded a BJ for not finding out the sex. This is all your fault. If she dumps me as a patient 'cause of you and your dick, I will not be happy."

"She won't dump us," he confidently says.

"And how do you know that?"

"'Cause I'm a Vanderbelt and if she dumps us, I will ruin her. You deserve the best and she's the best. Now, let's get out of here. You owe me a blow job."

QUINN

THIS BABY IS SO close to being born, and I'm freaking out, like big time. Hendrix has been amazing, but I'm concerned raising a baby at school will be, well, difficult. Who wants to hear a baby scream at 2 a.m. when you have exams the next day? I know I wouldn't if it was someone else in my predicament.

Sitting back, I sigh, and when I look up, I see people staring at me. Their gazes drop from my face to my belly and back again. Some smile when they get busted but others, like the group of football assholes who are currently staring, sneer at me or walk past and call me a 'slut' or ask me to meet them behind the bleachers. To quote Cher from *Clueless*, "Ugh, as if."

"They're staring again," I whisper to the girls while we finish our lunch.

Remy growls and seeing her so protective makes me smile. I was such a bitch to her when she first arrived. I'd heard the guys talking about her and totally misjudged her. I should have known better because the guys were being their Lordy asshole selves when it came to her arrival but they underestimated Remington Hearst, we all did. And now, she's dating Thatcher and she and I are great friends. She spins around in her seat and turns her glare at the guys staring at me like I'm a weird experiment. They turn their attention to her, and I see the moment she loses it, she pushes her chair back and storms over to them.

"If you don't keep your eyes to yourself, I'll make you eat them after I shove them up your ass and scoop them back out with a rusty spoon," she snaps at them. "Show some fucking respect."

Rowan snorts trying to cover her laugh, while Alani just lets it rip and bursts out laughing.

She walks back over to us and leisurely sits down, not a care that she just took on the football fuckers. "What?" Remy asks, picking up her fork and digging back into her salad.

No one says anything. We just smile at our friend until Alani breaks the silence. "Oh, nothing, but I have to say, when you threaten violence it's kinda hot. Too bad I love dick too much to turn to the other side." She winks at Remy and together they laugh.

"Quinn, don't worry about them, they're idiots. They clearly are forgetting who the baby daddy is, because if Hendrix were to catch wind of people staring at you and sniggering insults, he'd end them."

"Yeah, I don't want my baby daddy to end up in jail. This is already cliché enough as it is so let's not let him find out."

But fate is a fickle bitch, and my eyes widen when I hear. "Find out what?" I'd recognize that voice anywhere and when I look up, I see my baby daddy looking all sexy in his school uniform. *I wonder if we have time for a quickie before the next period?* Hendrix places his food tray down, and before he takes a seat, he kisses the side of my head and that need to fuck him intensifies. *Why is he so swoony today?*

"Nothing," all us girls tell him at once, and then we burst into another round of laughter just as Thatcher, Saint, Reign, and Hudson join us. The four of them give us all puzzled looks.

"They've all gone mad," Hendrix states, then bites into his burger.

"That happened long ago, dude," Thatcher says before he leans over and licks the side of Remy's face, earning himself a slap to the arm.

"Eeeew, Thatch, that's gross," Remy complains, wiping the side of her face with the back of her hand.

"You love it when I lick you, Peach."

"I do, but not my face and not in the middle of the cafeteria. You can lick me behind closed doors."

"Fine," he huffs, and like Hendrix, he chomps into his burger like a starving man.

Looking across the table, I smile when I see Alani and

Hudson making googly eyes at each other while Reign, oblivious to his partners eyes fucking each other, digs into his own burger. *Wonder if I have time for a burger too?* Then I notice down the other end of the table, sitting away from the rest of us, is Saint and Rowan. The two of them are having a hushed conversation and the look on both their faces worries me. Rowan hasn't been herself lately, and I feel like such a shitty friend. I've been so caught up in the baby and my 'who's the daddy' dilemma that I haven't been there for her. I vow to be a better friend, but first, I need one of those burgers the guys are eating.

Pushing myself up, I waddle over to the kitchen and grab a burger and some fries because you can't have a burger without fries, that's just not okay.

Sitting back down, Hendrix groans, "God, will you two get a room?" Looking up, I see him glaring at Hudson and Alani who have just pulled apart, their lips swollen and red from sucking face just now. I try to hide my smile because as nauseating as it is, it's cute. I'm glad they can't get enough of each other.

Just to pile on, Reign reaches over Hudson, grabs Alani, and pushes his tongue inside her mouth. After kissing her passionately, he licks her face just like Thatcher did to Remy moments ago. His actions earn him another groan from Hendrix, and I see the moment he decides to keep taunting his brother. He turns to Hudson and with Alani watching them intently from Hudson's other side, he kisses him and it's H O doubt T hot, especially when Alani leans in and nibbles Hudson's neck.

When Hudson, Reign, and Alani pull apart all eyes are on them, my pregnant belly forgotten by everyone in the room.

"What?" Hudson questions, looking around our table and the room.

"Nothing," we all say at the same time, and I might add, we all sound breathless.

Reign's eyebrows furrow slightly. Everyone is fine with him being bi-sexual so his look is one of confusion. He opens his mouth to ask again, but Thatcher jumps in.

"Seriously, it's nothing."

Not wanting him to feel awkward, I add, "That was H O double T hot," and I pretend to fan myself.

Hudson gives Reign's arm a squeeze, and Alani blows him a kiss, and just like that, the three-way kisses are forgotten and we go back to our usual chatter and ribbing, the awkward moment forgotten.

"Hey, man, how's it going?" Hudson asks Rian as he sits beside him with his own burger, and then I remember mine and dig in. Moaning as the beef juices explode on my tongue and through my burgergasm, I hear Rian's reply.

"Yeah, good, I guess. After all the craziness, life is settling down and it's good, really good."

"What up, fuckers?" Hart sing songs as he slides up next to Rian, pushing him into Hudson.

"Do you want to sit in my lap?" Rian laughs.

"Nah, you're not my type." Hart smiles, and then something interesting happens while I watch him. Theon joins us, sitting next to Remy on the other side of the table, and Hart's eyes follow him until he joins the conversation.

Alani notices too. She catches my eyes and mouths, "What was that?" and wiggles her eyebrows.

"You good, babe?" Hendrix asks, pulling me from watching everyone.

Placing my head on his shoulder, Hendrix kisses the

side of my head, and closing my eyes I murmur, "Yeah, I'm good and this is perfect."

I never thought I'd be in this situation in my last year of school, but life has a funny way of turning out just how it needs to be. As I look around our friend group, we've all been through our own drama and some, but at the end of the day, we are a family. We will all be there for one another, and you can't ask for more than that.

After lunch, we all split up and head to our last classes for the day. By the time the final bell rings, I'm utterly exhausted and as I make my way up to my room, I find myself once again thinking over the whole raising a baby at school dilemma.

"Baby?" Hendrix voices, kneeling in front of me while I sit on the bed. Staring blankly at him, I can't find the words. "Quinn, baby, I know something is bothering you."

Sighing because I know he's not going to stop questioning me, I put on my metaphorical big girl panties, and I spit it out. "I'm concerned ..." But I drift off, what if he tells me I'm being crazy?

"About?" Hendrix asks, taking my hand in his and squeezing, silently encouraging me to be honest with him.

"About the baby and school and raising him here. I mean, as amazing as Crestwood is, I'm not sure raising a baby here is the right fit."

Hendrix eyes me and starts to nod. He bops the tip of my nose and then gives me one of his signature smirks. "Leave that to me, I'll sort it out," he says. "I have a plan."

"Huh? How? What are you up to?" I question because I'm not sure he's taking my concern seriously. Like how can he have a plan when I just voiced my concern thirty seconds ago?

"Quinn, don't stress, baby. I got it. You just get some rest, you're exhausted."

And he's right, I am exhausted. I'm even too exhausted to argue with him. Doing as I'm told, I lie down like he suggested, but before I can ask him more questions on how it's sorted, my heavy eyes begin to shut. The last thing I see is Hendrix scrolling on his phone beside my bed, and I wonder what he's up to.

HENDRIX

AFTER SPENDING the evening with my brothers, I let myself into my room and smile when I see Quinn is here. She's on the bed fast asleep, snoring softly. Her hand rests protectively on her belly.

I'm wide awake right now, and as much as I want to slide into bed and sink myself into her, I know she needs her rest so I find something to keep myself occupied. I get to work and put together the bassinet I bought recently. Once it's all together, I begin to unpack some of the baby things, but because I'm a squirrel brain right now, I can't focus on one task.

Opening one of the bags Remy and Thatcher gave us, I chuckle out loud when I see what's in the gift bag. Quinn makes a noise behind me and I freeze that I woke her. Peeking over my shoulder, I sigh in relief when I see she's still fast asleep.

I continue rummaging through the bag and realize Remy may have gone overboard. Our baby will definitely be the best-dressed kid in Crestwood, even if he's the only kid in this school. Then I remember Quinn's concern from the other day and smile when I think about what I've been secretly doing behind her back. I can't wait to show Quinn, I just hope she doesn't kill me.

Pulling out countless more outfits—all designer of course—because our baby deserves nothing else, they are a Vanderbelt after all, I come across a sweater embroidered with my last name.

Vanderbelt.

Fuck, it hits me like a freight train. I'm going to be a daddy.

Me, Hendrix Vanderbelt, the black sheep of the family is going to be responsible for another human being.

Reaching inside, I smile when I pull out the matching pants and beanie.

Warmth fills me and excitement bubbles to the surface. Looking back at Quinn, her belly is exposed slightly from when she rolled. I lift to my knees and spin around. I gently place my hand over her stomach, my fingers splayed across her skin, and I feel a gentle thump against my palm. My eyebrows raise because it's the first time I have felt her kick without Quinn prompting that she's just started her acrobatic lesson for the day.

Leaning forward, I place a kiss where my hand is, whispering, "I'll always be here, Tootsie. Daddy will always be here, no matter what. You and Mommy are it for me."

Needing to be close to her, I kick my shoes off and climb in behind Quinn.

Pulling her to me, I rest my hand across her belly and snuggle, holding her and Tootsie closely. This baby will only ever know love, I will never treat my child the way my father treated me and my brothers. One day, Tootsie is going to be one hell of a little Vanderbelt.

… one week later

"What are you up to, Hendrix? And why do I have to wear a blindfold?"

Normally on a Saturday morning, I would prefer to still be back at school naked in Quinn's bed, but I was up super early this morning and then I woke her and demanded she get dressed. The demands continued, and when we got to the car I thrust the blindfold at her. I may have growled for her to put it on.

"You'll find out very soon, Quinn, 'cause we're almost there. And as for the blindfold, keep it after this because I have plans." I lower my voice and add, "Dirty sexy plans."

"Do tell," she asks, and I notice her wriggling in her seat at the thought of my sexy plans for us and this blindfold.

"Well, Quinn, I'm picturing you splayed out on our bed, naked. Your wrists and ankles are cuffed to the bed frame, and your eyes are covered."

"Hendrix," she breathlessly pants, "I cannot go wherever we are with damp panties."

"You can always take them off," I offer, earning myself a smack in the arm and I'm impressed she hit me square on. Then I panic that she can see, but before I can dwell on it, I arrive at our destination.

Turning the car off, I look at the house before us, and I smile. Taking a deep breath, I look at Quinn. "You ready?"

"Ummm, maybe." Her voice is shaky. "If I didn't know you like I do, I'd think you've brought me somewhere to kill me."

"No chance of that ever happening 'cause I love you, Quinn Ellis."

"I love you too. Now, can I take this blindfold off?"

"In a sec." Without another word, I climb out and round the car to her side. Opening her door, I take her hand in mine and guide her out of the vehicle. "Out you come, baby momma, but be careful."

"If you unblindfold me, I could be more careful. Just sayin'."

"True but trust me, this will be worth it, and for the record, I'll always look after you, Quinn. Always. And again for the record, you look sexy blindfolded."

Placing a kiss on her temple, I pull her away from the car, and together, we walk over to the entrance gate.

Standing behind her, I lean in. "You ready?" I whisper.

She nods, and I pull the blindfold off and place my hands on her hips. I now wish I could see her face, so I step to the side and watch her as she takes in the house before us.

"This … this," she stammers, "this is just like the one I wanted when I was thirteen."

"This IS the one you wanted when you were thirteen."

She looks around and when she sees the park down the street, she gasps and covers her mouth. "You remembered," she mumbles, her eyes welling with tears.

"I remember everything, Quinn, and I distinctly remember you telling me that one day, you wanted to live here, and well, the other day when you said you don't really want to raise a baby at school, I made your dream happen."

She turns to face me, and I can't tell if she's happy or sad, but when she throws her arms around my neck and slams her lips to mine, I think I did good. As if she's in my head, against my lips, she says, "You did good, Vanderbelt. But how did you do this so quickly?"

"I have my ways. Now, wanna head inside and look at our new house?"

"Yes, and once we've looked around, I'm going to give you a 'thank you, you're amazing' blow job, and then I need you to make love to me."

Nodding, I quickly agree to her terms.

Lacing my fingers with hers, I open the front gate and we walk down the path and up the stairs to our new home.

QUINN

"WOULD you like to do the honors?" He offers me the keys to our place. Nodding and with a shaky hand, I take the keys from Hendrix's palm and insert the key into the keyhole. Turning the brass key, I unlock the front door to our first home together

Our

flipping

house.

I'm seriously in shock he did this. It was only last week I voiced my concerns about having Tootsie at school and then BAM, he once again swoops in and saves me.

I've loved this little navy blue and white two-story American farmhouse since I was thirteen. It has flower beds running along the front veranda. On the porch at one end is a swing I can now picture Hendrix, Tootsie, and I sitting on, watching the sun set over Crestwood. There's a navy blue door with a solid brass handle. Beyond the exterior, I have no clue what it looks like on the inside, but I'm sure it will be just as gorgeous.

Pushing the door open, I'm about to step over the threshold when Hendrix swoops me up into his arms, bridal-style, and carries me over the threshold. "Welcome home, Quinn," he whispers as he presses his lips to mine. Placing me down on my feet, I drape my arms over his shoulders and kiss him back.

In the doorway of our new home, we kiss like teenagers on a Saturday night. Breaking the kiss, I pull back and smile up at him. "This is amazing, Hendrix. How the fire truck did you pull this off?"

"I have my ways," he cheekily says, and I eye him. "If you must know, I got to know the owners. One day I was walking by and Mrs. Snow was working in the garden. She looked up and we got chatting. I told her how you loved this place and that one day I was going to buy it for you." Holy swoon, Batman! "A few weeks ago, I got word that Mrs. Snow had a fall and was in hospital. Mr. Snow was already in a home, he has dementia, and he was too much for her to handle. Last week, I went to see her after you broke down about raising Tootsie at school. I asked if I could buy it for you so that me, you, and Tootsie could live here."

"And she sold it, just like that?"

He nods. "Yep, she sure did. Her fall made her realize it was time for her to move into the home with Mr. Snow. It's almost like fate intervened and made it a possibility. We do have to have her over for afternoon tea once a month, but you'll like her."

"Who knew big bad Hendrix Vanderbelt was such a softie?"

"Shhh, don't tell anyone, I have a reputation to uphold."

"Your secret is safe with me. Now, let's explore our house."

Taking his offered hand, we walk into the living room. Off the living room is a doorway that leads you to the open-plan kitchen and dining area. The kitchen has granite countertops and shaker cupboards in hues of black and off-white. There's a farmhouse sink that looks out into the backyard where I can see a gazebo with a built-in outdoor kitchen and a pool. "It has a pool?" I squeal in excitement. Opening the French doors that lead outside, I step onto a small patio and look over the yard. It's huge and not what I expected to find back here. Not only is there a pool and the gazebo, but there's also a jungle gym and hot tub.

"We are gonna have some awesome parties here," I excitedly tell Hendrix. Then my eyes widen. "We need to have a housewarming."

"That can be arranged, but first, let's explore the rest of our house."

Nodding, we head back inside where we find a half bath, two bedrooms with a jack-and-jill bathroom, and a study. Up on the second floor are three bedrooms, one of which is the master, and a main bathroom. Stepping into the master bedroom, my eyes widen when I take in the room. It's huge, it must take up half of the second level. There's a walk-in closet that rivals the one Big built for Carrie in *Sex and the City,* and an en suite bathroom that I never want to leave. A double shower and a claw-foot tub in front of the window look that overlooks the backyard.

"I cannot wait to have a bath in that," I tell Hendrix.

"I can't wait to fuck you in that shower. It even has a built-in fuck seat."

"I don't think that's the technical term, Mr. Architect."

"Fuck seat, shower seat, same, same," he says with a shrug, and I can't help but smile ... or press my legs together as I imagine myself straddling Hendrix and riding him on our fuck/shower seat.

Laughing at his reply, I shake my head and stare over at him leaning against the doorway. He's wearing cargos and a charcoal Henley with the sleeves pushed up to his elbows. My gaze rakes over him, and that pulse between my thighs intensifies.

Lifting my gaze to his, we stare intently at one another. The temperature in our en suite is rising by the second. "We should christen the shower," I suggest.

Hendrix grabs his shirt at the back of his neck and pulls it over his head in that sexy-as-hell way I love, and I'm ready to come there and then. He raises his eyebrows in a 'you have too many clothes on' kind of way and with my eyes locked on his, I begin to undo the buttons down the front of my sundress.

One by one, I pop them open. When enough are undone, I slide the straps down my arms and push the material over my hips. It flutters to the tiled floor, leaving me in my ballet flats and an orange G-string.

"You are sexy at the best of times when naked, Quinn. But when you are pregnant and naked, I have no fucking words."

"I'm not naked," I remind him. "I'm still wearing my panties."

He stalks over to me, grips my panties in his huge hand, and tears them from my body. The flimsy material disintegrates from the force and he raises his eyebrows at me. "You're naked now," he matter-of-factly states.

"I am, but we have another problem," I inform him.

"And what might that be?"

"You have far too many clothes still on."

"That's an easy fix." Quicker than *The Flash*, he strips off, leaving him as naked as me. He slides his hands around my lower back and lifts me off my feet. He stalks into the shower and turns the faucets on. A squeal slips out when the cold water hits my skin but a few seconds later, it's warm and the shower stall is filling up with steam.

We stand under the spray and stare at one another. "I do believe I owe you a 'thank you, you're amazing' blow job." Before he can protest, I drop to my knees before him. Looking up at him, I grip his shaft and give it a few pumps as the tip leaks precum. Swiping my finger through it, I bring my finger to my lips and moan as his salty cum dances on the tip of my tongue. Opening my mouth, I suck and swallow his dick. The tip hits the back of my throat, causing me to gag a little. Moving my head back and forth, I pump and suck him. Lifting my hand, I massage his balls and feel them tighten in my palm. He's close.

Hendrix pulls me off. "The first time I come in our house, I want to be balls deep inside you."

He helps me up and sits on the shower/fuck seat. He grips his shaft, and with his eyes locked on mine, he beckons me forward. Walking over to him, I straddle his lap and rub the tip of his dick up and down my slit before I sink myself down on him. Moaning, my pussy hugs his dick.

"Your pussy is like heaven," he tells me as I ride him harder.

Sex has always been great with Hendrix, but now that we are officially an us, it's out of this world amazing. He kisses me deeply as my release builds.

With each thrust, I'm closer to detonation.

With each lash of his tongue, a new high washes over me.

He breaks the connection and stares at me. I feel his gaze deep in my soul and my love for him simmers in my blood.

"Suck my tits," I demand.

"Yes, ma'am," he replies.

Kissing down my neck, my head drops back, and he makes his way to my boobs. Lifting his hands from my hips, he caresses my tits and takes my nipple into his mouth.

It's just what I need, and I scream his name as pleasure explodes inside of me. Every nerve ending and cell comes alive as I ride out my release. My orgasm sets Hendrix off and he comes too, grunting and groaning as he release inside me.

We wash up and climb out, and when he hands me a towel, I giggle.

"You got orange towels," I whisper as I bring the fluffy orange towel to my face and breathe in.

"I know how much you love hideous orange towels and I want you to feel at home here."

"You should feel at home, too," I tell him.

"I do, look." He holds up his towel, a black one.

Thankfully orange and black go together and I can't help but laugh.

Once we are redressed, me sans panties because

someone shredded them, we head downstairs and when we step into the kitchen, I pause mid-step because I see all our friends and an array of foods on the counter.

"Surprise," they all shout when they see Hendrix and me.

For the rest of the afternoon, we hang out at home. Home, I love saying that.

I have the most amazing boyfriend. We have an amazing house and cannot wait to decorate the nursery and bring Tootsie home.

Life could not be more perfect, and I'm one lucky lady.

HENDRIX

EVEN AFTER ALL THE family drama, I'm on cloud fucking nine right now. I'm going to be a dad and Quinn and I have moved in together, and not five minutes ago, did I get the best fucking blow job from Quinn. I mean, they're all good, she seriously is the best head giver. This baby has the best mom, I just hope my DNA doesn't fuck her up.

Fuck, this baby has Vanderbelt DNA because I'm the dad. I have been glowing since that revelation and I could not be happier. Rounding the corner, happily humming to myself, my mouth twists into yet another smile, but it immediately drops the moment I hear my brother growl, "I told you to not fucking touch her again."

Saint's voice echoes around me, and I'm confused by his words, but also ready to go to bat and assist him. Not wanting to show myself, just in case he has this handled, I peek around the corner and catch my brother's fist raised and his other arm holding Mr. Ashford against the wall.

Smirking at Saint, Mr. Ashford sneers, "And I told you to mind your fucking business, Vanderbelt. She's my fucking daughter, and I will do what I please … I can always punish you as well, and we both know, I'm much harder on you."

I'm ready to step in and help Saint, but I stop when I see him quiver. Even though Mr. Ashford is the one pinned to the wall, it's Saint who is shaking, but he shakes that off and in the blink of an eye, his fist flies into Mr. Ashford's face.

From where I'm hiding, I hear the crack of his nose, and I can see the spray of blood clearly as it spurts out, covering them both.

Fuck, I should stop this from happening, but I'm enjoying the way Saint's giving Mr. Ashford a work over. I'll wait a few more moments and see how this plays out. My money is on Saint hitting him again and I'm all for it. Mr. Ashford is a cunt, not Thornton Vanderbelt cunt level but a cunt, nonetheless.

Saint stands over a bleeding Mr. Ashford, fisting his shirt. He's in full-on angry Saint mode now. He pulls Ashford up so he's right in his face and headbutts him. He throws him to the floor where he lies there semi-conscious, blinking up at Saint.

Saint towers over him. "You ever lay a fucking hand on my girl again, I'll chop your fucking dick off and feed it to you. You're done abusing her and me," Saint sneers, shoving him back to the ground. "Fucking done, it ends now."

What the fuck? Abuse?

Saint stalks off. He's so angry he passes by me and doesn't see me. Slinking out, I look back at Ashford who is still lying there, and it takes everything I have to not beat the fuck out of him, but right now, my brother needs me. I follow close behind him and catch up in no time. My fingers grip his upper arm. He spins to face me, fist raised and ready to fight, but when he sees it's me, he drops his arm and nonchalantly says, "Hey, bro."

"Don't 'Hey, bro' me. What the fuck was that back there?" I bark, gesturing to where he left Mr. Ashford.

"Nothing," Saint snaps and turns away from me, continuing on like nothing just happened.

"Nothing my ass," I shout. "Bro, what the fuck did I just witness?" I stop him again, gripping his arm tighter this time.

"Just leave it, Hendrix."

"Leave it, just leave it," I sneer. "You just all out accused Mr. Ashford of abuse and you're telling me to leave it. Did he fucking touch you?" I hiss, ready to go back and give the fucker another round. With my entire body shaking I turn, not waiting for Saint's reply because I'll get an answer from the asshole himself.

"Wait," Saint mutters. The tone of his voice stops me in my tracks. Turning to face him, I'm ready to go to war for my brother, but when I see his face, that anger returns, and the need to pummel Mr. Ashford is strong.

"Motherfucker," I growl. Turning, I sprint back to where Mr. Ashford was but he's now surrounded by a crowd. Saint rips me back, shoving me into the wall before I can make a scene.

"I have it handled," he hisses.

"Handled, you call that handled?" I point my finger to where Mr. Ashford is being helped up. I watch as he's practically carried through the hall, students and teachers staring after him wondering what the hell happened. Saint glances in his direction before his glazed eyes snap back to mine. Stepping over to him, I grip his face in my palms and rest my forehead against his, forcing my brother to look right at me. "You, me, Thatcher, Reign, we're in this together. One in, all in, nothing else matters."

Saint takes a gulp of breath, trying his best to control his emotions, as tears slide down his face. I tug my brother into my arms, Saint is a part of me, one-third of me, we're in this together.

He mentions needing to get back to Rowan, so I let him go to her as I need to get back to Quinn. Even after all the fuckery my father caused, there's still more drama at Crestwood. I never thought Saint would be involved with something like this, but then again, I never thought something like that would happen here. I'm almost to Quinn when it hits me that I can't even talk to Quinn about this because Rowan is her best friend. *Fuck*, have they even spoken about it? Does she know what's happened and has been keeping this from me?

Fuck.

Before he leaves, I promise Saint I'll keep this news to myself—for now—he knows as well as I do I can't keep this a secret forever. Thatcher and Reign will want to know, and once they do, together, as brothers, we will get our revenge on that slimy fucker, but for now, I'll give him time, but I won't keep this secret forever. He will tell them, or I will.

QUINN

… just before graduation

"OH MY GOD," I complain. "I hate being pregnant," I tell Remy as she sits next to me in the library.

She does her best not to laugh out loud, but it escapes her anyway. "I'm sorry." She smiles. "But you love it and it suits you. You're glowing. Your tits are amazing and in a few short weeks, you'll have a beautiful baby boy."

"Boy?" I question.

"Yep, my baby senses are telling me boy, and you

cannot change my mind on that. Remington Vanderbelt has a good ring to it," she proudly says.

"Yeah, not sure Remington will be his or her name, but I have time to come up with a perfect one."

"If you go with Remington, you are set whether it's a boy or a girl."

"Besides, when you and Thatch get hitched, you'll become Remington Vanderbelt and, personally, I think one Remington Vanderbelt is enough in this group," I say, laughing, and she joins in too.

"Yeah, you might be right," she says and then adds, "and that also rules out Thatcher, Reign, Saint, Hendrix, Hudson, Rian, and Theon."

A sharp pain shoots through my stomach, and I take a breath, interrupting her. This is a pain like I have never experienced before, and I have to bite my tongue to try to control the urge to swear. This is the second one since we got to the library, adding to my lower back pain over the last day or so.

"Quinn," Remy asks, her tone worried. "Are you okay?"

Nodding, I grimace when another sharp pain shoots through me again, but this time I can feel it lower. My eyes widen when suddenly my pants and seat are wet, very, very wet.

My look of shock catches Remy's attention, and she murmurs, "Quinn?"

Looking down, I move my legs slightly feeling the dampness between them. I'm used to damp panties, hello, Hendrix is my man, but this is different and then it hits me, and my already wide eyes widen farther. "I … I think," I stutter and take a deep breath, "I think my water just broke."

"What?" she shrieks, gaining the attention of the other students around us and a glare from the librarian.

Rushing to my side, she helps me up and I do my best to move as fast as I can, but the pain becomes too much and I have to stop just as we get to the library doors. I'm doubled over as another tearing pain rips through me. I begin to panic because I know the closer to birth I get, the stronger the pains are going to be, and it already hurst like a bitch. I need the hospital and all the drugs, and as if she's in my head, she literally voices what I just thought.

"Come on, we need to get you to the hospital so we can get you the good drugs," Remy says, gripping my hand to help me through the doors.

"Yes," I tell her, "I need all the drugs." I cry out again as another contraction hits with the force of an F5 tornado. *Why do women go back a second time? This is shit.* This one forces me to bend over once again and hold my stomach. Remy tries her best to help me, but she's just as tiny as me, well, I was as tiny as her before I became the size of a beached whale.

"Come on," she urges me, her voice laced with panic.

"Remy," I whisper-cry, "I can't. I can't." Tears streak down my face because it's too much. "I need Hendrix," I cry.

"You can do this," she encourages and helps me farther along the hall just as Reign and Lennon come around the corner.

"Shit, Remy. Quinn, are you guys okay?" Reign asks, but he's a clued-in guy who knows what's happening and is already pulling out his phone. "Get here right now. Library." He all but screams down the line at who I assume is Hendrix.

Reign and Lennon take over from Remy. I cry out again

and rather than continuing to the parking lot, they help me into a classroom on the lower level.

The door slams open, and Mr. Ashford lifts his head from his desk and glares in our direction, giving us a ridiculous look.

"Can I help you?" he sneers. I really don't like this man, but he's my best friend's dad so I've never voiced it aloud.

Groaning, I grip Reign's hand, squeezing tightly as another contraction hits. He grunts, breathing through the pain and if I wasn't in the midst of labor, I'd laugh at the big bad Lord cringing over a hand squeeze.

My contractions are about two minutes apart now. "This baby is coming," I mumble to no one in particular, and that's when I notice Mr. Ashford, with the help of Remy, is setting up a space on the floor for me to give birth.

"Where's Hendrix?" I groan, gripping Reign's shirt and growling my question in his face.

"He's coming," he says.

Nodding, I let go of his hand, and for the first time since the contractions started, I feel okay knowing Hendrix is on his way. I cry out when another one hits and again, I grip Reign's hand, hearing a soft, "Fuck me," escape him.

"Quinn?" I hear Hendrix shout before he bursts through the door, immediately coming to my other side. "Fuck, Quinn, this wasn't the plan." If I wasn't in so much pain right now I might just nut punch him. Hendrix takes my other hand, and I breathe through the pain. The Vanderbelt brothers each hold my hand as I work my way through another contraction.

"Okay," Mr. Ashford says from down between my legs.

"What the fuck?" Hendrix growls. "What are you doing down there?"

"Delivering your baby," Mr. Ashford says to the room.

"Like fuck you are," Hendrix hisses, and I don't recognize him or his tone right now.

"Do you know how to deliver a baby?" Mr. Ashford asks calmly. Hendrix shakes his head and lets him continue, but I feel rage coming from him.

"What the fuck?" Saint's voice booms from the doorway.

"Quinn's having the baby," Remy states, pulling him in next to her and holding on to his arm, but Saint is trying to pull free from her grasp. I have never seen Saint so angry before.

"Not fucking him," Saint growls while at the same time, Lennon asks, "Uh, man, do I need to stay?" His face has lost all color, and he looks like he's going to pass out.

"Get the fuck out," Hendrix all but shouts.

Lennon hightails it out of the room.

Remy comes up behind me and slides her legs on either side of me. She uses her body as back support and holds me against her. "We've got you," she says into my ear and when I look over my shoulder, I see her smiling.

"Thank you," I whisper.

I'm already exhausted and I haven't even pushed yet. I really wish I was in a hospital and had all the drugs.

Saint moves in beside Reign and kneels. His gaze collides with Mr. Ashford's and they share a look I can't decipher. Saint growls, "One wrong move and I will end you." Their stare-off is interrupted when I scream as another contraction hits. This time it feels like my vagina is about to rip in two. My entire body feels hot, and I'm sweating to the point I could start an indoor pool.

"Deep breaths, Quinn. You got this, baby." Hendrix kisses my temple. Closing my eyes, I take a few deep breaths, for once listening to him and trying to remember what I learned in the baby classes.

"Okay, the baby's close. I can see the head," Mr. Ashford says, causing my eyes to snap open and panic to seep in again.

I'm going to be a shit mom because I wasn't even aware I was in labor. I had slight back pain this morning and the odd flutter, but I assumed it was Braxton-Hicks.

"Okay, Quinn, on the next contraction, I need you to push," Mr. Ashford says.

Nodding, I wait, and a few seconds later, I squeeze my eyes shut and almost break the boys' hands when I push and push, letting out an exasperated sigh when I finish.

"One more," he tells me. Breathing through clenched teeth, I squeeze down on Hendrix's and Reign's hands, giving everything I have to getting this baby out of me.

By the third push, I'm exhausted and ready to give up. Leaning back on Remy, I cry as exhaustion takes over. My eyes begin to grow heavy as fatigue sets in, I just want to sleep.

"Quinn, baby, come on, you can do this," Hendrix tells me when I whimper as another contraction hits.

Mr. Ashford says, "Push!"

I bear down and give it everything I have, when suddenly a cry fills the room, and a gasp escapes me. "I did it," I blubber, "I did it," repeating the statement again.

Saint removes his shirt and hands it to Mr. Ashford. He uses it to wrap my baby up then hands the baby to me and places it on my chest. "It's a boy," he says while Hendrix and I stare down at our baby.

Mr. Ashford stands and moves away, giving us space.

A sob falls from my lips, and I stare down at our son. Hendrix and I have a son.

Reign and Remy both move away, leaving Hendrix to move in behind me. The three of us huddle on the classroom floor, and we bond with our new baby.

"Hey, little guy," I whisper softly. He begins making a noise that is music to my ears, I lean down and kiss his little face. He calms slightly, and I swear he smiles, even though I know that's not possible when he's only a few minutes old.

"Hey, Ellis," Hendrix says.

Looking up at him over my shoulder, a puzzled look mars my face. "Really?" I murmur.

Hendrix nods. "He's a part of both of us, so he's Ellis Vanderbelt." Tears fall down my cheeks and I kiss Hendrix. He runs his finger down Ellis's face, and again, I swear he smiles at us.

"Hey, Ellis, I'm your daddy and this here is your mommy. We love you so so much, and we promise not to fuck you up."

But suddenly our moment is interrupted when Saint yells and punches Mr. Ashford, hitting him right on the jaw. "You son of a bitch," Saint growls.

Reign grabs his arms, holding him back. "I need help," Reign shouts, doing his best to hold back an enraged Saint. Hendrix jumps up to help Reign hold Saint back, and Remy moves in, coming to my side.

Mr. Ashford holds his jaw glaring at Saint.

"Calm down, Saint. Calm the fuck down," Hendrix hisses at his brother.

"No, fuck that. I'm done hiding." Saint pulls free and steps into Mr. Ashford's space again. "You're a fucking asshole," he yells at Mr. Ashford. Remy and I share a puzzled look just as Thatcher, Hudson, and Alani all enter.

"What the hell?" Thatcher states, then his eyes widen when he sees the baby in my arms, and Saint growls, literally growls, baring his teeth at Mr. Ashford.

"Saint?" Thatcher murmurs, moving toward him.

Saint is erratic and shaking. He's holding back his tears, and finally, I watch as one falls down his cheek. He bats the droplet away and then murmurs a statement that shocks us all, "He..." He points to Mr. Ashford. "...has been abusing Rowan for years ... me too."

Both Reign and Hendrix drop Saint's arms, sharing a look between them.

"Come again?" Thatcher snaps, but then he turns his deathly glare to Mr. Ashford. "You touched my brother?" Thatcher growls.

"No!" Mr. Ashford states.

Thatcher snaps his gaze back to Saint, who shakes his head. Taking a deep breath, he collects himself. "Physically not sexually." There's a collective sigh at that news. "But Rowan wasn't as lucky," he says, scowling at Mr. Ashford. "He physically, emotionally, and sexually abuses her, but it stops today. You may have delivered my nephew, but it doesn't make up for the abuse."

The room falls silent. "Someone needs to call an ambulance ... and the police," I voice.

Remy nods and makes the calls. Taking her hand, I smile to thank her, and then there's movement in the doorway, and when I look up, I see Rowan standing there. The room once again goes silent. She looks at me and Ellis and smiles, but then she looks over at Saint. I can tell the moment she realizes her secret is no longer a secret, and as I lie here with Ellis in my arms, I feel like a shitty friend for not being there for my friend. How did he get away with it for so long? And why did she never tell anyone? Or at least tell me?

My moment of why is interrupted when she whispers, "Saint." Her tone is broken. He stalks over to her and pulls her into his arms, kissing the side of her head. He tugs her into his chest, shielding her from Mr. Ashford.

Rowan cries as he holds her, and I find myself crying along with her. I look down at my new baby and vow to always be there for him. I feel so much love for him already. In an instant, he's the most important person in my life. Ellis will always be my number one, no matter what. I'd die for my child, and it hurts that Mr. Ashford couldn't do the same for my friend.

SAINT

TODAY HAS BEEN A CLUSTERFUCK, but at the same time, it was filled with joy. Quinn gave birth to my nephew, officially making me an uncle. Seeing that little boy wrapped in her arms for the first time caused something inside me to snap, and I spilled my guts. The thought of anyone touching that little boy the way *he* touched Rowan was the straw that broke the camel's back, but now I worry Rowan will hate me for outing us once all the emotions of today have settled.

I'm pacing back and forth in Rowan's room. Our emotions are both high, and when the adrenalin wears off, we are going to crash, but I need to be strong for her. We are in this mess now because I spilled my guts.

We've both just given our statements to the police and the school board. The angst I feel about it finally being over is nothing compared to what I feel knowing that it's no longer our secret. Everyone knows.

Fuck, everyone knows.

Me and my big mouth revealed it all, but I don't regret it. That lil' baby made me confess to it all.

"Saint," Rowan whispers.

"I'm right here, Dove," I state, smiling over at her. She's curled in a ball on her bed, her fingers fidgeting with a thread on her quilt. "He's where he should be," I say, knowing what she's thinking.

She sniffs and nods in agreement but doesn't say anything else. I hate not knowing what she's feeling or thinking right now, and I know I need to give her time, but it sucks. It sucks big hairy donkey dicks.

"I'm sorry," I voice as I climb onto her bed and shuffle behind her. Wrapping my arms around her, I repeat my apology over and over. She shakes her head and rolls over to face me. She places her hand on my cheek in that reassuring way. Covering her hand with mine, I stare at the strongest woman, next to my mom, that I know.

"It's okay, Saint," she murmurs. "You've always protected me, and I know you did what you did today to protect Ellis." She pauses. "You're always protecting me."

"And I always will," I honestly tell her.

The day she first confessed to me after I discovered what I discovered, was the lowest day of my life. I wanted to kill Fuckface Ashford. I wanted to go to the authorities. He was assaulting the sweetest person in the world. His daughter for fuck's sake. But she'd made me promise to keep it to myself, she didn't want anyone to know, so instead, I vowed to protect her and keep her secret that soon became our secret. I'd let him use me so she didn't have to do it anymore.

My scars are only physical. But Rowan's, fuck, hers are physical and emotional. They are deep, and I will be here for her every step of the way. She's never fully told me how long he's been doing it, but I know it's longer than I think, but I won't push her.

Taking a deep breath, I let out a sigh. I know we have to eventually face everyone, but for now, I like our little bubble. We've kept to ourselves since yesterday, choosing to hide away, but the need to see my brothers and new nephew is strong.

Fuck, I have a nephew and I haven't held him yet.

Thatcher and Hendrix were beside themselves, being triplets and not knowing what was going on with me must be killing them. They feel like they've betrayed me some-how, that they broke some secret triplet vow, but they didn't. My brothers *have* tried to talk to me, but I wasn't ready to share.

The moment we step outside these walls, everything will change. Everything will be different. The moment I spilled our secret, Rowan and I became the talk of the school. Everyone forgot Arlen killed my father or that Hudson, Reign, and Alani came out as a throuple. The news of Hendrix and Quinn having their baby at school didn't even make the news because this is so much more. This is the juiciest thing Crestwood has right now, and because of me, my Dove has to face the music. I want nothing more than to hide Rowan away so she doesn't have to face our peers. Face the looks and the questions and most of all the whispers. I don't want Rowan to face that because she's been through enough, and now, I have no clue if she's truly going to be okay.

My phone vibrates on the side table, reaching over to grab it, I know it's bound to be one of my brothers checking in.

HENDRIX

> Come meet your nephew. We're in my old room.

"You had to go there," I mumble, and now I feel like a horrible brother. Hendrix is a new dad. He has a son, and I'm an uncle, yet I'm hiding away in fear of what other people will think.

"I want to hold him," Rowan says, reading the text Hendrix sent me.

"You're sure?" I ask, trying my best to sense if she truly wants this.

"Quinn is my best friend, she just had a baby, and I haven't even seen him yet. As much as I'd love to stay in here forever with you, we need to face them all eventually, Saint." She pauses and then adds, "We can't hide forever."

I scoff, "Try me, baby." I smirk. "I will happily hide away with you for the rest of eternity." My comment earns me a smile and when Rowan Ashford smiles, the world shines brighter.

She reaches up and cups my cheek. "Together," she softly whispers.

"Together," I whisper back, earning myself another mega-watt smile.

Texting Hendrix back, I tell him we'll be there in ten.

Pulling her up, I hug her tightly and then we get ready to go meet my nephew. Hand in hand, we walk the short distance to my brother's room.

Lifting my hand to knock, I look down at Rowan and smile just as the door flies open revealing Hendrix. As soon as he sees us, a relieved expression appears on his face. He reaches out and pulls Rowan and me into his embrace.

Rowan slips out of his arms, and then he tugs me back in for another hug. He murmurs into my ear, "I'm here," and hugs me tightly again.

Squeezing him in return, I clap his back, giving him a silent thank you. Pulling back, I slap my hands together. "Now, let me see this nephew of mine because the cool uncle has arrived."

QUINN

EPILOGUE

… three months later

SITTING ON THE PORCH SWING, Ellis is cradled
in my arms sucking on my boob, and Hendrix is shirtless
in the yard. We are redoing the front path, well the whole
front yard. A wicked storm went through here a few
weeks ago and the gorgeous gardens Mrs. Snow had
maintained for over forty years were wiped out. Crestwood got slammed by what the weather people are calling

an inland tsunami, resulting in a deluge of flooding, rain, and damage.

It's kind of a blessing in disguise because we wanted to put our own stamp on the place so we ended up pulling everything out, including the path and we're starting again ... with the assistance of Mrs. Snow. The only thing we kept was the front fence and entrance, that stone fence and archway were going nowhere.

Hendrix swipes the sweat on his forehead and even all sweaty and gross, he's hot.

"There's a little something on your chin," Rowan teases as she sits down next to me. That's another development, she and Saint have moved into one of the downstairs bedrooms. Shit went down at school, and I swear we were living in an episode of *Days of Our Lives*. While the dust settles, the two of them are hiding out here.

I'm glad my friend is here and I can finally be here for her. When it all came out, I, well, all of us, felt like shit that we were unaware of what had been happening right under our noses.

"You okay?" I ask her, reaching over and taking her hand in mine.

She nods but doesn't smile. She is far from fine but we as a family, as our chosen family, will ensure that both her and Saint are indeed fine again in time.

"Ummm, you have something on your chin." It's my turn to tease her, but I don't blame her. Saint is just as abtastic as my man.

"Hands off, he's mine," she playfully growls.

"Girl, he's all yours. I'm happy with my very own Vanderbelt."

"You two, right there, ogling us while we slave away in the hot sun?" Hendrix calls out.

"Yep," Rowan and I call out at the same time, and then we fall into a fit of giggles.

Ellis stirs and falls off my boob, causing milk to spray everywhere—I'm like a Jersey cow at the moment, I have been since my milk came in at the hospital—and breast milk sprays all over Rowan. She squeals and jumps up, causing both Hendrix and Saint to race toward us.

"Oh. My. God. You milked me," she cries out just as Saint leaps over the railing like he's Chris Hemsworth in an action movie.

"Ohhh, shit, Quinn," Saint calls out, covering his eyes. "Put your tit away."

"It's just a boob," I tell him and to taunt him more, I squeeze my nipple, mainly to see if I need to switch Ellis to the other, but it sprays more milk and I know it's not time to switch yet. Ellis cries out and I reattach him. He happily snuggles back into me and suckles on my tit again. Seems Ellis is a boob man like his daddy, but then again, my tits are amazing at the moment.

Hendrix walks up the front stairs and joins us. He stares at Ellis sucking my breast and heat fills his eyes. "Later," I mouth. He nods and places a kiss on my temple.

"Okay, now that we know it was just a nip slip and not a spider or a murder, let's get back to it. Everyone will be here in a few hours, and I would like to have the path done so they don't track dirt and mud all through the house."

"Look at you being all Mr. Domesticated. Dad would be rolling in his grave," Saint says, pouring himself a glass of water.

"He can get stuffed. Maybe if he gave a damn, he wouldn't be dead."

"He'd still be dead and rather than Arlen, it would

have been Mom. To be honest, I always thought she was the one to off him."

"Me too," I say, agreeing with Saint. "You need anything before I get back to it?" he asks me.

"Nope, we're all good, but hurry, 'cause after this, Ellis will be down for at least three hours and well ..." I waggle my eyebrows at him.

"We'll be done in an hour."

"Deal," I tell him.

He and Saint get back to it and just over an hour later, a dirty Hendrix walks into our bathroom. I'm soaking in the tub, and when I see my sweaty and sexy man walk in, my clit immediately throbs. This bath is big enough for the two of us and on many occasions since we've lived here, he and I have had a fun afternoon, or evening, in the tub.

Hendrix strips off his pants and stands there, staring at me surrounded by bubbles. My body is now thrumming, and I need him to get into this tub and fuck me now. "You better hurry up and get in here, I still have to prep for the party tonight, but before that happens, I need your dick in my vagina."

"Those fuckers can wait for us, it's our house and it's our party. Besides, if I want to fuck my fiancée, I'll fuck my fiancée."

"One problem, I'm not your fiancée."

Walking over to the tub, he drops down to one knee and produces a solitaire diamond ring. "Quinn Ellis, you are the light of my life. The pain in my ass. The mother of my child. These past few months with you and Ellis have been the best of my life, and I don't ever want to stop feeling like this. Will you do me the absolute honor and become my wife? Marry me, Quinn, and make me the happiest man in the world?"

Holy fucking shitballs. Hendrix Vanderbelt just asked me to marry him. He just asked me in the most unromantic of locations but his words were ohh so romantic, which makes up for doing it while I'm naked in the bath.

Standing up, water sluices down my body, and in my haste to get out, I slip, but Hendrix is quick and manages to wrap his arms around me, saving me—again—before disaster strikes.

"Shit, Quinn, are you okay? And are you rushing to get away from me because the thought of spending the rest of your life with me warrants your death?"

"Are you stupid? I'm racing to say yes, so much yes. You surprised the shit out of me, that's all but, Hendrix, I would love to marry you." Throwing my arms around his neck, I slam my lips to his, kissing him deeply. "And FYI, the answer will always be yes when it comes to you." He smiles at me and I have never felt so much joy. Pressing my lips to his again, I start to kiss him and then I remember the ring. "The ring," I mumble against his lips.

Pulling back, Hendrix takes my left hand and slides the ring onto my finger. It fits perfectly. "It looks good," I tell him. "But you know what will look better?"

"What?"

"My hand with my ring, wrapped around your cock, pumping up and down."

"And you know what would look even better?" he throws back at me.

"What?"

"Your fingers sliding into your cunt and the diamond shining in the light."

"Like this," I coo and rest on the edge of the tub. Spreading my legs, I slip my hand between my thighs, I slide my middle finger down my slit before pushing it inside.

"Fuck, that's hot." He drops to his knees between my thighs and focuses on my diamond-clad finger moving in and out.

Leaning forward, he sticks his tongue out and licks up my slit to my clit, circling his tongue around the sensitive bundle of nerves. Closing my eyes, I focus on the sensation of my fingers and his tongue.

"Eyes open when you come," Hendrix demands. They flick open and I look down. He has his eyes on me and never has he looked more sexy. He winks at me and bites on my clit. That's the detonation I need and I come, squeezing his head between my thighs as I ride his face and my fingers.

He rises to his feet, and I pull my fingers from my cunt. He grabs my wrist and brings my digits to his lips. He sucks and licks my fingers clean. "I love you, Quinn Ellis, and I cannot wait to marry you."

"I love you too, Hendrix Vanderbelt, and I cannot wait to marry you, but first, let's finish our bath and seal the deal with an engagement fuck."

HENDRIX

EPILOGUE

WELL, that went better than planned. I knew she'd say yes, because well, Quinn and I are a forever kind of thing but the events after were amazing.

All our friends and family are here for a barbecue, and it's the perfect time to announce our news to everyone, but first, we need to attend to our little man.

We hear Ellis stirring through the monitor and Quinn stands up and heads inside. She's only been gone a few minutes, but I miss her so I jump up and follow her.

Walking upstairs, I head toward the nursery and lean against the doorframe, watching my fiancée—I love saying that—feed our son.

"You just going to stand there like a creeper or are you going to come in?" she asks, lifting her head to stare at me instead of the little bundle sucking on her boob.

"I'm good with being a creeper, and guess what?"

"What?" she asks, smiling at me.

"I get to be a creeper for the rest of my life now, and I'm okay with that," I honestly tell her.

"Guess what?" she throws back my question, and I cannot wait to see what her reply is.

"What?"

"I'm okay with you being a creeper for the rest of our lives. Me and you against the world, Vanderbelt. Now, come give me a kiss and then pick out an outfit for Ellis because I want to tell everyone our news when we get back down."

"You know," I tell her, "I'm surprised the girls didn't notice your new bling when they got here."

"Me too, but I think your mom did."

"Well, she may have helped because that ring there on your finger was her mom's."

"Hendrix," she cries, her eyes welling with tears. "That's so sweet. You really are the best."

"I know," I cheekily tell her. "But there's more." I go over to Ellis's closet and I pull out the onesie I got made for the occasion. "So, I went to Mom the week after Ellis arrived and told her I wanted to marry you. She was thrilled because she loves you and Ellis as much as I do. Then we put a plan together for me to propose. I didn't mean to do it while you were naked in the bath, but we never do anything the traditional way so." I shrug. "But to commemorate the occasion, I also got this."

Pulling out the onesie, I turn it around to show her, and she chuckles. It's a bright Quinn orange onesie and in black lettering it says,

My Mom and Dad Are Getting Hitched!

"Hendrix," she cries again, "this is perfect. You are perfect, and if Ellis wasn't sucking my tit right now, I'd blow you."

"We have a lifetime for blow jobs, Quinn. Now, hurry up so I can announce to the world you're mine."

"We have news," I declare when we walk back downstairs after Quinn finishes feeding Ellis. Ellis is in my arms, and my fingers are laced with Quinn's, leaving her left hand free to show the world.

Everyone stops what they're doing and looks at us.

"Soooo," I draw the word out, suddenly nervous to share the news with everyone. "Quinn and I ..." But before I can finish, she lifts her left hand and wiggles her ring finger. I quickly spin Ellis around so everyone can read his onesie and together we shout, "We're getting hitched."

Everyone is silent and I begin to think they aren't happy for us when the room erupts into applause. The girls all squeal and my brothers grin and shake their heads.

"That'll be one hundred," Reign says to Thatcher. "Told you he was going to propose within six months."

"Eat a dick, you asshole," Thatcher throws back at him before he jumps up and pulls Quinn and me in for a hug.

Congratulations are passed around and Mom breaks out the bubbly. With her being in on my plans, she helped arrange the celebratory drinks.

"I'd like to make a toast," Mom says when everyone has a glass in hand. "Not only did Hendrix make me a grandmother, but he also officially gave me a daughter." She looks to the other girls. "You ladies will officially be my daughters too one day."

"Yeah, when my loser brothers step up and ask," I tease.

"Hendrix," Mom scolds, and my brothers tease me that I got in trouble.

"Sorry, Mom, continue."

"As I was saying, I'm a grandmother and now I have a daughter. Our family is growing and I could not be happier. This year has been tough, but we are Vanderbelts, and no one fucks with us."

My brothers' and my eyes widen at Mom's choice of words, but they are true. We are Vanderbelts. We are the Lords and you don't mess with us … or our women.

"To Hendrix and Quinn," Mom says, rounding out her speech.

Everyone raises their glasses, and our casual barbecue becomes an unofficial engagement party.

The girls get straight into wedding planning, and my brothers and I sit back and watch them. If you'd told me this time last year that I'd be a dad and Quinn and I were engaged, I'd tell you to put down the crack pipe, but a lot can happen in twelve months, especially in Crestwood.

My heart is full right now and I cannot wait to see what happens next for me. I never dreamed I'd get my happily ever after, but here I am. I'm engaged, and I have a perfect, happy, and healthy baby boy. Life is grand and I feel like a king.

THE END!

Want to find out what happens next? Well, you can in Saint, the 4th and final book in the Lords of Crestwood Prep series.

SAINT

This is our school, our kingdom.
My brother's and I rule, we are The Lords.
Secrets never stay secrets so I shout mine from the rooftop.
That was, until her—Rowan Ashford.
We kept our secret close but now? Everyone knows what we were hiding.
Now that it's out, the road ahead is unknown.
Nothing is as it seems but we have each other, we'll be fine. Right?

SPOTIFY PLAYLIST

Bad Guy - Billie Eilish
It's You - Ali Gatie
Havana - Camila Cabello feat. Young Thug
Blow - Ed Sheeran feat. Chris Stapleton
Lips On You - Maroon 5
Mood Ring - Britney Spears feat. Ape Drums
Sweet Melody - Little Mix
I Knew You Were Trouble - Taylor Swift
New Boy - Samatha Jade
Lights Down Low - MAX
Piece Of Work - Loren Gray
Hard For Me - Charley
Bad Boy - CARYS
B.O.M.B - emlyn
Beautiful Creature - MIIA
M.I.A - Cher Lloyd
Never Really Over - Katy Perry
Afterlife - Hailee Steinfeld
Queen - Loren Gray
I'm Ready - Sam Smith. feat Demo Lovato
Blood, Sweat & Tears - Ava Max
In My Bed - Sabrina Carpenter
Chaotic - Tate McRae
Best Part Of Me - Busby Marou
Happier Than Ever - Kelly Clarkson
Ruin My Life - Zara Larsson
Wave - Meghan Trainor feat. Mike Sabath
Boys Like You - Anna Clendening

This playlist can be found on Spotify.

ABOUT TARA LEE

Tara Lee is an Australian author who writes spicy romance, and men to swoon over. She comes from Hobart, Tasmania where she lives with her husband and two children.

When she's not a stay at home mum wrangling her two small children or fighting the voices in her head to be quiet she's getting up before the sun rises as a qualified baker.

Tara is a Pisces who survives on energy drinks, chocolate frappes and busting moves at Jazzicise for some me time.

ALSO BY TARA LEE

PLEASANT GROVE SERIES

Taking chances

Second chances

New beginnings

THE BEAUTIFUL SERIES

Beautifully Broken

Beautifully Mine

Beautifully Damaged

STANDALONES

Chance Encounter

HARLING HILL DUET

We All Fall Down

We End With Us

All of these books are available on Amazon.

ABOUT DL GALLIE

DL Gallie is from Queensland, Australia, but she's lived in many different places all over the world, including the UK and Canada. She currently resides in Central Queens- land with her husband and two  munchkins. She and her husband have been together since she was sixteen, and although they drive each other crazy at times, she couldn't imagine her life without him.

Shortly after her son was born, DL began reading again. With encouragement from her husband, she picked up the pen and started writing, and now the voices in her head won't shut up.

DL enjoys listening to music, drinking white wine in the summer, red wine in the winter, and beer all year round. She's also never been known to turn down a cocktail, espe- cially a margarita.

ALSO BY DL GALLIE

STAND ALONES

Antecedent

Doc Steel

Oops

Off the Books

Fractured:A driven world novel

Deck...the Balls

Secrets and Sunrises

Always in the Cards

Out of Nowhere

Love Me Like You Do

Never Let Me Go

Seven Nights

Seven Kisses

Before the Ashes

After the Ashes

PUCKING NOVELS

I Pucking Hate That I Love You

A Pucking Good Christmas

…and a few pucking more

FALLING NOVELS

These men make it hard not to fall for them

Falling for Dr. Kelly

Falling for Dr. Knight

Falling for Agent Cox

Falling for Agent Cruz

Falling:The Complete Collection

THE UNEXPECTED SERIES

When it comes to love, expect the unexpected

The Unexpected Gift

The Unexpected Letter

The Unexpected Package

The Unexpected Connection

The Unexpected series: The Complete Collection

THE CASTAWAY GROVE COLLECTION

Love has arrived in the Grove

Oasis

Unequivocal Love

Five Words

Broken Rules

…and a few more to come.

The Castaway Grove Collection, Vol 1

THE LIQUOR CABINET SERIES

Liquor has never been so disturbingly saucy

Malt Me (Book 1)

Tequila Healing (Book 2)

Wine Not (Book 3)

The Final Shot (Book 4)

The Liquor Cabinet: Series boxset

All of these books are available on Amazon.